I0456893

The Elder Chronicles

Volume 5

Elder Escape

By

Robyn Kelly

This story is fiction. The settings are imaginary. Any resemblance of the characters or places to actual persons or places is purely coincidental.

Table of Contents

Prologue

The Elder Council had deemed it necessary to teach the current generation of inhabitants something of Elder history. The shaman, Red Hawk, who had participated in much of that history, had been convinced to return to the Valley to hold periodic seminars on the more critical events. The talks were being recorded so that future generations would have a first hand account of their history.

The word quickly spread throughout the Valley after Red Hawk's first session with the Elders. This time there were over fifty children and adults present and the group had taken over the entire Council chamber. Red Hawk waited patiently in a trance until they had all settled down and a silence came over the room. Then Red Hawk began speaking in a slow but steady voice …

"At our last session I told you how I toiled to become a shaman so that I would be able to visit your Valley and how Enela returned from capture by a couple of humans. Ari-Ana took me under her wing and taught me much about your people and about life in the Valley. I began to help Ari-Ana with children passing through puberty. Then I graduated to assisting some of you with searching your earliest memories. Ari-Ana was looking for some hint as to your origins and how you came to this planet. But, try as we might, neither she nor I had been able to learn anything of any consequence.

"During that period I led three lives. On weekdays I was Dr. Joanne Archer, clinical psychologist at the Winton hospital. After work and on weekends I visited the Valley as Red Hawk and worked with Ari-Ana. And in my spare time I continued studying with Gray Wolf, the tribe's shaman and my mentor, and assisted him with the local tribe. My husband thought I had given up on him completely.

"When my daughter, Patricia, was born, she became the center of my life and all other considerations went away. Unlike Elder children, human children are totally dependent upon adults for their survival and education. In human society, the parents usually perform this role. The human mother bears the child and is the person primarily responsible for its care. The father simply provides the sperm necessary for conception. He will usually provide the family with the necessary income to survive. Any additional services are seldom offered and rarely performed well.

"So it was that I left the Valley for some time. But Ari-Ana and I continued to meet on several occasions, just so that I might keep up with the happenings in the Valley. I had asked Ari-Ana if Patricia would have to become a shaman before she could visit the Valley. She assured me that it would not be necessary and that I cold bring her with me whenever I came to visit. Patricia would be the first human child raised, at least in part, in an Elder environment. It was during those visits that I learned of Enela's further adventures and together we discovered the origin of the Elders.

"Enela was a true Elder child, but she had been kidnapped as a baby by the man who killed her mother and was raised as a human child. That peculiar mix of environment and heredity made

Enela a very unique individual. She successfully passed through puberty with the assistance of Ari-Ana. But instead of becoming a typical Elder adult, she became a typical human teenager. Listen now as I tell you of Enela's great adventure and her remarkable contribution to the Elder people."

Chapter One

The Rebel

Enela was bored. Since she was now considered an adult among the Elder population, she had been assigned certain chores to perform. None of the Elders really had to work hard, and most could choose the jobs they wanted. But Enela did not want to do any job. When she had protested once too often Ari-Ana had taken matters into her own hands and had assigned her a couple of the more unpopular jobs. She was to tend to the condition of the various toilet holes and ensure that they were functional. She was also to inventory all of the supplies in the storage chamber and maintain an accurate list of available items.

There were a total of eight toilet pits scatter around the perimeter of the Valley. Watching over the toilets kept Enela out in the open and allowed her to travel all about the Valley. It was a fairly easy task and Enela really didn't mind it at all. If the toilet was overfull, she would flag it so that the Elders would not use it. In a couple of days she would stop by again and remove the flag.

The inventory was another matter. The supply chamber was a large underground chamber in the center of the Valley. In it was stored everything that the Elders had found useful at some time during their stay on Earth. Nothing was organized, so that finding what one wanted could take forever. Trying to arrange everything kept her cooped up in the supply chamber and was a bear of a task. Elders were always coming in to borrow something or to bring something back. But they never put it back where they found it. When Enela came across something that was out of place, she never knew if it was a new item or one that had been misplaced. She would have to go back and recount all like items. Then she didn't know if one had been borrowed in the meantime. It was all very confusing and she was getting nowhere fast.

When Enela complained to Ari-Ana the latter simply told Enela that she could solve her problem if she would just apply herself. Enela decided that maybe a break from the action would be more promising. She knew that she was not supposed to leave the Valley without the permission of a Councilor, but Enela yearned for a taste of the great outdoors.

So she took the only avenue that was readily available to her. She retreated to the steep, narrow path that led to the top ledge of the butte. The Council always had two or more guards posted on the top of the butte. Their job was to keep a watch for any humans attempting to gain access to the butte, or flying over it at a low altitude. (The area west of the reservation road had been declared a no-fly zone. No aircraft were authorized to approach the butte below 30,000 feet.)

The job of guard was a lonely one and the regular guards rather enjoyed Enela's sojourns to the top of the butte. But Enela was not really interested in conversation, she liked to lay back and look at the sky, or to watch the surrounding desert, or just to relax, away from all of the activity in the Valley below. That simple act seemed to release all her tensions and strengthen her connection to her past.

Whenever Ari-Ana needed Enela for anything, or to remind her a some scheduled appointment, she would just send out a mental message. But to be truly effective, such messages had to be directed in the direction of the recipient. Ari-Ana had become accustomed to Enela not responding. When there was no response, she suspected she would find Enela on top of the butte. At first, she tried to excuse Enela because of her past. Then she tried to counsel her. At last she had even tried punishment. Nothing had worked.

Any normal Elder would simply accept whatever chore was assigned to them and keep at it until it was completed. Ari-Ana was becoming reconciled to the fact that Enela was just not a normal Elder. "Perhaps," Ari-Ana thought, "she never would be."

One day, after a particularly frustrating morning in the supply bunker, Enela fled to the peace and serenity of the top of the butte. She plopped down at the southern end of the butte and looked out over the desert landscape. Another smaller butte a mile to the south was in her field of view. At one point in time, Enela knew, another Indian tribe had lived in caves the dug into the wall of the butte. The river that now flowed beneath her butte once flowed on the surface just west of the other butte.

As Enela watched, a cloud of dust appeared in the distance. She had never seen a dust cloud there before. Enela watched as the cloud approached.

"Umia!" Enela called out to one of the guards lolling nearby. "Take a look at this!"

The guard wandered over, squinted at the dust cloud, then turned and started to wander off.

"Wait!" Enela called out. "Don't you think we should report this?"

"We were briefed to expect an incursion of humans at the south butte," Umia responded laconically. "They have permission to gather around the other butte. As long as they don't try to come over here, we are not to be concerned."

"What are they doing here?" Enela was no longer in panic mode, she was just curious.

"Don't know and don't care," Umia said as she returned to her resting place.

Enela, still curious, lay back down and watched as the dust cloud neared the butte, then began to dissipate. The angle of the butte blocked her view of what was going on. Occasionally, she would see a human come into view and then disappear again. The doings at the other butte had Enela's rapt attention. She did not even sense Ari-Ana approaching her position.

As she approached, Ari-Ana motioned to Umia to be quiet. Once she was standing directly behind Enela, Ari-Ana looked out to see what was so interesting. Then she reached down and tapped Enela on the shoulder.

"What's so interesting?" Ari-Ana said quietly.

Enela immediately recognized the voice and flipped over so quickly and violently that she almost fell over the edge of the butte. She stumbled to her feet and bowed to Ari-Ana, but any sensible response escaped her.

Ari-Ana was greatly enjoying Enela's reaction. "Don't you have a job to do?" she suggested.

Enela nodded and was desperately looking for a way to escape back to the supply bunker, but Ari-Ana was completely blocking the narrow pat along the top of the butte.

Ari-Ana realized what the problem was and moved back against a rock outcropping allowing Enela just enough room to squeeze by. She watched as Enela raced back to the path to the Valley below and disappeared into the distance. Umia was on her feet and bowing as Ari-Ana followed Enela.

Chapter Two

The Dig

Enela really did try to keep up with her job in the supply bunker. But it was too boring and too frustrating. She couldn't help her mind from returning to the activity at the other butte. Even a good night's rest didn't take her mind off what she had seen. "Maybe," she thought, "just a little peek would solve her problem."

There were never many Elders in the south area of the Valley near the passage through the butte wall. Most of the Elders preferred the north end of the Valley, which was covered by a dense forest of pine trees. It was a simple task for Enela to get to the passage unobserved and sneak through it. She emerged into a canyon in the outer butte wall where Gray Wolf's cabin was located. His horse was missing from the corral, but she still hugged the wall of the butte and tried to remain out of sight until she was well away from the cabin.

Enela's goal was the top of the other butte just to the south. From there, on a clear day, she could see the town of Winton farther to the south and the Indian town of Wakulla to the east. It was a great place just to sit and think. Maybe, if she could just get up there and have some time to think, she could figure out her inventory problem. At least she could solve the mystery of what was going on behind the butte.

Enela ran easily across the desert, maneuvering around the various plants and adjusting her body to the heat of the day. Her skin effectively reflected any harmful UV rays, so the bright noonday sun was of no concern. In less than fifteen minutes she had reached the butte and began the climb to the top. Unlike the butte that surrounded the Valley, this one had suffered some calamity in its past. Part of the eastern side of the butte had collapsed leaving a great pile of rocks that reached almost all the way to the top. Enela looked around carefully as she climbed. She could not afford to be seen by anyone, especially by some human who might be in the vicinity. There was no one in sight and Enela quickly finished her climb.

Once at the top, Enela moved to the southern edge and sat down, gazing out at Winton far in the distance. She just enjoyed the view for a few minutes and then cleared her mind to focus on her task. Before she could get started, she was startled by voices coming from the base of the butte. Human voices, from what she could make out. Enela shifted to a prone position and looked down over the western edge of the butte. There was a group of humans down at the bottom. Some were standing around while others seemed to be digging in the ground around the butte. Enela watched for a while. It was all most curious.

The area of the reservation west of the road was supposed to be 'sacred ground' None of the local Indians would ever come out here and no other humans were supposed to be here either. Now, Enela could observe several vehicles parked just south of the butte and a group of humans walking around the western side of the butte.

Enela had visited this butte often. The ancient riverbed west of the butte was still partially visible. The western side of the butte had at some time in its past housed a tribe of cliff dwellers. No one remembered just which tribe it was, but the caves they carved into the butte were interesting to investigate. There was also a large gathering place on the ground in front of the caves where it was presumed the inhabitants prepared food, ate and held ceremonies.

The local tribe kept the area in fairly good repair and sometimes led paying tourists from Wakulla to the site. But these people did not look like tourists and there were no signs of any Indian tour guides anywhere in the vicinity. Enela continued to watch, but could not quite make out what the humans were saying. She decided to go down to the first tier of dwellings. She could still be out of sight and could perhaps learn what was going on.

Enela worked her way down the north side of the butte and then maneuvered around to the edge of the dwellings. She took great care to stay out of sight of the humans on the ground. She found a spot on the first ledge where she could lay down and watch the people below. She could also hear bits and pieces of the conversations.

"When do you think the professor will be back?"

"He said he had a luncheon meeting; probably some time around two."

"Found anything, yet?"

"A few pottery shards. I think Randy found a bone."

"God, it's hot out here!"

"I'm going to get another bottle of water. Anyone want anything?"

14

"A cold shower would be nice!"

"I'd settle for an arrowhead!"

Enela could see squares of string laid out on the ground, with humans digging in some of them. Then the fog parted. This was laid out like some kind of an archeological dig. But no serious archeologist would waste any time on this worn out location. These must be students from the college in Winton.

As Enela watched, most of the humans seemed to coalesce in a spot next to the butte. There was a lot of talking and joking among them. Enela couldn't figure out what was going on. Then it dawned on her. It was noon. They were just taking a lunch break.

It was all very fascinating, but she couldn't safely stay any longer. She did have work to do. And if Ari-Ana caught her out here, her hide would be stored in the supply bunker – permanently. She made her way back to the rock slide and started to climb down to the desert floor.

In the distance Enela saw a lone rider approaching from Wakulla. It was probably Gray Wolf on his way home. Now she really had to hurry to get through the canyon before he arrived at his cabin.

Chapter 3

Who Are You?

Over the next couple of days, Enela would make her way to the top of the butte only to observe that Gray Wolf's horse was in his corral. With Gray Wolf in residence, she did not dare to try to sneak out of the Valley. On the third day, though, the way was clear.

Enela made her way out of the Valley and over to the southern butte. She again went up to the top of the butte and crawled over to the western edge. All of the activity seemed to be going on directly at the base of the butte. Enela couldn't really hear or see much from the top of the butte.

Finally, she decided to get closer to the action. She made her way to the north end of the butte and down the rock slide until she was level with the lowest ledge on the south face. She carefully made her way out onto the ledge. It was again lunch time and there was a group of young people gathered around the tailgate of a station wagon. They were obviously enjoying lunch.

Enela was fascinated by the scene playing out down below. She didn't pay any attention to what was going on just behind her.

"Hi, there! Enjoying the show?" Enela froze in mid breath. Someone was standing right behind her. When she recovered her senses, she rolled over slowly and looked back. There, standing in the door of one of the caves was a young human female. Enela just looked at her, her mind racing, trying to figure out what to do next.

"My name is Mary," she said casually. "Professor Gauss is my father. Who are you?" Mary spoke in a quiet voice tinged with curiosity.

Enela couldn't think of a good lie right off, so she opted for a little bit of the truth. "My, my name is Enela," she sputtered.

Mary continued to lean against the doorway, but she was eyeing Enela with even greater curiosity. It was obvious that she was not in the habit of stumbling across hairless nude females with white opalescent skin among the ruins.

"Is there a nudist camp around here that I don't know of?" Mary was still curious. "Or do you just not like clothes?"

"Actually, I don't like clothes," Enela replied. "I don't wear any clothes unless I have to for protection."

"If some of those guys down there see you, you'll wish you had a suit of armor," Mary offered. "They're jocks looking for an easy 'A'. They are pretty crude and always seem to have sex on their mind. I'm only 16 and they have already tried to hit on me – when my father wasn't around." Then she got curious again, "Do you live around here? I know I haven't seen you here before."

"I live out in the desert," Enela was careful not to say where in the desert.

"I know this area pretty well, " Mary said. My father drags me out to these digs because he doesn't want me to hang around Winton alone when he's not there. I have explored a lot in my free time. You must be new."

"Yes, I'm new," Enela answered weakly.

"Hey! Who are you talking to, Mary?" a voice cried out from below. "You got a boyfriend up there with you? Where's Tommy?"

"Let's go see what's so fascinating up there!" another male voice suggested.

"You better just stick to your digs!" Mary shouted down, coming out from the doorway.

"C'mon, guys," the first voice said. "Somethin's up!"

"Yeah, maybe she needs protection!"

"No. You're the ones who'll need protection. A female voice chimed in as several of the boys headed for the cliff.

"Oh, they can't find me here!" Enela exclaimed, jumping up. She forgot for a moment that once she was standing she would be visible from the desert below the butte. "I've got to get out of here!" She turned toward end of the ledge where it met the rockslide.

Mary hesitated for a moment, then said, "You can't go that way. That's where the ladder is. Come with me!" She turned and went into the room behind her.

"I can't go there," Enela protested. "They will find me for sure."

"Just get in here and do what I tell you," Mary insisted. She took hold of Enela and pulled her into the room.

The room was only dimly lit by the sun. There was no other exit and nothing to hide behind. Mary went to the back of the room and just stood there for a moment. Enela could hear the boys' voices coming closer. They were already on the ledge. Suddenly, the wall in the back of the room split open. Before Enela could even get a grip on what was happening, Mary grabbed her and pushed her through the opening, whispering, 'Trust me!" The wall closed behind her and Enela was left in total darkness.

Within seconds the boys burst into the room, demanding to know what was going on. Mary protested that there was nothing going on. That she had simply been looking around the ruins as she often did. Some of the boys insisted that they had seen someone up on the ledge with Mary. They knew she had been talking to someone. Mary simply shrugged and suggested they look around to their heart's content. She was the only person there. Randy pinned Mary back against the wall and shoved his leg between hers. He had a gleam in his eye that indicated he definitely had something sexual on his mind. He tried to kiss her, but whatever he intended, was cut short by a yell from outside.

"Professor Gauss is on his way back!"

The professor had issued strict orders that all the students were to stay out of the ruins and concentrate their efforts on their respective digs. He was well known on the campus as being a strict disciplinarian. None of the boys wanted to waste their summer by flunking this particular course, so they quickly made their way to the ladder and back to the ground. Even Randy decided that a tryst with Mary would not be worth an 'F' in the course; and he quickly retreated with the others.

Mary breathed a deep sigh of relief. She had no desire to lose her virginity to a sports jock like Randy. It was only yesterday that she had felt the pangs of ovulation, and she hadn't yet started on the pill. "No," she thought. "Definitely not with Randy."

Then Mary remembered Enela. She did a quick scan out the door to make sure that the boys were indeed back on the ground. She could also see the plumes of dust being raised by her father's vehicle as it approached the butte. She went back into the room, to the back wall, and felt with her toes for the patches of loose dirt. She found the levers hidden there and pressed down hard with both feet. The wall split open, and Enela, still somewhat dazed, came out into the relative brightness of the room. Mary pushed on the walls and they closed with a soft click.

"Thank you, I think," stammered Enela. "What just happened?"

"Those dumb jocks would have had us for dessert," Mary explained, "if my father hadn't picked this time to return. That stupid Randy almost raped me as it was."

"Are you all right?" Enela was genuinely concerned. Rape never occurred among the Elders, but Enela knew of it from her time with the humans.

"I'm fine," Mary assured Enela. "But you really need to get out of here. Now that my father is back, he'll be wanting to tell me I shouldn't be up here, either. If he were to see you the lid would really blow off! Can you get back down the way you came?"

"Yes, no problem." Enela said. "You go on back down the ladder to attract their attention and I'll use the opportunity to get off the butte."

Mary did as Enela suggested while she slipped past the ladder to the rock fall. Enela did not waste any time trotting back across the desert to the entrance to the Valley. She was only mildly surprised when she arrived back at the storage bunker and was told that Ari-Ana wanted to see her.

Chapter 4

Danger Threatens

Ari-Ana was seldom in a good mood where Enela was concerned. This afternoon was no exception. Enela found her waiting in the Council chambers. Enela knew that she had misbehaved badly and decided to face the music as contritely as possible.

"You wanted to see me, Ari-Ana," she said with a deep bow as she approached.

"What am I to do with you, Enela?" Ari-Ana added a little extra guilt, just for good measure. "I know very well that you abandoned your task at the supply bunker, that you left the Valley without permission, and that you could easily have been seen by humans. Any one of those is a serious enough offense, but you have managed to rack up all three in the space of a single afternoon!"

"I'm sorry, Ari-Ana, I just don't know what came over me." Enela tried to sound as convincing as possible, but she wasn't sure that she was succeeding.

"I'm sure I don't either, Enela," Ari-Ana was using her sternest voice. "I have tried to take your human upbringing into consideration and give you the benefit of every doubt. But this is not the first time you have gone off on a wild adventure. What do *you* think I should do?"

"I don't know, Ari-Ana." Enela was beginning to get just a little frightened. Ari-Ana was sounding, and looking, unusually stern. She was afraid that her punishment was not going to be just another slap on the wrists.

"No it will not be another 'slap on the wrists'!" Ari-Ana was being very indignant. "Enela, meet Hila."

Hila stepped out of an alcove to one side of Ari-Ana. She was somewhat older and larger than Enela. She looked very muscular and had a very serious expression. The first thought that crossed Enela's mind was that of an 'enforcer' or bouncer.

"You are not far wrong, Enela," Ari-Ana continued. "Hila is going to be your constant companion for a while – perhaps a long while. She will accompany you everywhere. She will be your shadow. Should you even look like you're about to violate the rules, she will see to it that you don't. Oh, yes, she has strict instructions not to cripple you, or kill you in the process. I trust she will obey her instructions better than you have obeyed yours."

Enela would have turned a ghostly white, if she had not already been that color naturally. She might as well have been locked away in chains! There was no way that she was going to shake off Hila, and if she did manage that feat, it would surely be immediately reported to Ari-Ana. Enela didn't want to envision what Ari-Ana's reaction might be to that.

"Now," Ari-Ana was on a roll, "since your task at the supply bunker does not seem to adequately fill your time, I have another task for you."

Enela actually started to groan, until she realized what she was doing and immediately managed to stifle it.

"Beginning tomorrow," Ari-Ana was quite emphatic, "you will spend at least one afternoon a week with Ari-Red Hawk while she helps you explore your memory of the past. I expect her to report that you cooperated fully and willingly. That is all. You and Hila are dismissed."

The two young Elders bowed and quickly left the Council chamber. When they were sufficiently far away, Hila broke the silence.

"Look, Enela, I don't like this any more than you do. I had a nice cushy job as a weather observer before Ari-Ana tapped me for this gig. I really don't feel comfortable being an enforcer; but if that's what I am ordered to, that's what I will do. Can we start out at least by being friends?"

Enela gave the thought some serious consideration, but she wasn't ready to give in quite so soon. She just headed on over to the food cave to get some fungus to chew on while she pondered her options.

The next morning Enela was up early and went straight to the supply bunker. She had decided, for the moment, to ignore Hila. If she wanted to tag along, fine. But it wasn't going to matter to Enela one way or the other. As usual, many items had been returned yesterday afternoon and simply placed anywhere there was vacant space. It was the same muddle Enela found every time she started her job. No matter what she did, every day started with a new mess that had to be straightened out. By the time she got things organized, other Elders would be in for the things they needed and it would be impossible to do an accurate inventory. It was all very frustrating!

As Enela began to arrange things, Hila looked around and began to get the big picture. "Enela, while you are putting things back in order, why don't I stay here by the entrance and make a record of anything that is taken out. That way, when we start the inventory, we will know what is missing."

Hila's comment was like a satori. Of course! Enela thought. She had been far too focused on the details to see what the task required. It was all so simple! Hila made her record of the items leaving and Enela straightened up the others. When everyone had taken what she required, the two worked quickly to complete the inventory. It was finished shortly after noon. Then, after a quick break to relieve their bladders and slake their thirst, Enela and Hila sat down to work out a plan of action. As the two talked they became more and more eager to carry out the plan.

"We have two requirements," Enela pointed out. "First we have to have a complete inventory, then we have to have an easy way to recount every so often."

"Why don't we mark everything we have counted, so we will know that it has been counted?" Hila asked. "I think I saw an old can of paint in there. Just a spot of that should do the job."

"Okay," Enela said. "And suppose we arrange like things together with the things used most often near the entrance, do you think the Council would issue an order that people should put things back where they got them?"

"How come you want other people to obey the Council?" Hila asked with a snicker. "You don't exactly have a good track record in that department."

Enela threw a wig at Hila. But, in the end the two agreed to give it a try and spent much of the after noon rearranging items in the bunker. There were only minor disagreements about which items deserved to be closest to the entrance. When they had finished, they headed off to the Council chambers to report to Ari-Ana.

Ari-Ana was not in the Council chamber, but Red Hawk was, seated serenely on the floor obviously waiting for something.

"I'm glad you remembered our appointment, Enela," Red Hawk didn't sound too annoyed. "Shall we use this meeting room?" She indicated a small room at the side of the chamber. "Hila, you can wait for us here or tend to some other chore. We shall be a bit over an hour." With that Red Hawk ushered Enela into the room. There was no door to shut as the Elders observed intentional privacy as strictly as they enjoyed communal living.

As they were settling down Red Hawk asked, "Did Ari-Ana tell you what we are going to be doing?"

"Not exactly," Enela answered. "She said something about tracing my memory … "

"For years Ari-Ana has been examining the race memory of the Elders here in the Valley," Red Hawk explained. "She is trying to discover any information about the period during which your people arrived on earth. So far she has discovered only that the race memory stops at that time, which is highly unusual. Most of the Elders can relate stories they have heard of their

26

ancestors being able to remember things through several millennia. I am using my skill as a psychologist and a shaman to try to get around the problem."

"So you want me to remember things?" Enela was confused.

"Not exactly," Red Hawk continued. "When you use your race memory you usually just search for information on a specific subject. We don't yet know what subjects we want information on. So what I am going to do, with your permission of course, is to try to unwrap you memory, layer by layer, until we get to the time period we are interested in.

"We will begin by entering together into a trance and then start examining your most recent memories. When you come out of the trance you will not remember anything that we have done, but you will remember where we left off, so we can pick up at that point in our next session. Are you willing to assist me?"

"From what Ari-Ana said, I don't think I have an option." Enela was a tad bit sullen.

"We will get nowhere unless you willingly agree to participate," Red Hawk was quite calm and reassuring. "I will not force you. If you decide not to help me, I will simply tell Ari-Ana that we were not compatible and that the project had to be cancelled. She will accept that."

"How long is all this going to take?" Enela had worked with Red Hawk at the Tucson hospital when she was just Dr. Archer. She liked Red Hawk and trusted her, but this mind probe thing still bothered her. What if something went wrong, or her mind was somehow altered?

27

"We will meet for an hour or so two or three times a week," Red Hawk explained, "depending on my schedule." Red Hawk was still being very reassuring. But she also sounded determined. "I have never done this type of probe before, so I don't know how long we may be at it. We will stop when you run out of memory or you are no longer willing to continue. Shall we get started?"

"Okay, I guess so…" Enela did not remember anything after that point. She just seemed to be floating in blackness. It was neither uncomfortable nor frightening. She could not see anything nor feel anything nor smell anything. Every so often she could hear Red Hawk asking her a question or suggesting some object to remember. But she could not remember the comments. In what seemed only a few moments she found herself again sitting in the meeting room with Red Hawk.

"Is everything all right?" Red Hawk was asking.

Enela nodded, still not quite sure of what had just happened. "Did something go wrong?"

"Not at all," Red hawk smiled. "You responded quite well. But we are done for today. We will meet again in two days, if you are still willing."

Enela nodded somewhat foggily and they left the room to find Hila waiting for them in the main chamber. Enela and Hila went off to get some fungus for supper. Hila did her best not to seem too curious, but it was obvious that she was dying to know what had happened. Enela tried to explain, but discovered that she actually had no idea what had really transpired. It wasn't until they were quietly nibbling on their supper that Enela suddenly erupted, "Oh, piff!"

Hila almost jumped at the outburst, "What is it?"

"She must have learned about everything that happened on the cliff!" Enela sounded so worried and scared that even Hila began to be concerned.

"What happened on what cliff?" Hila's curiosity was showing, but she was still very wary.

"Yesterday I went to the pueblo butte to watch the humans at their 'dig'," Enela continued. "That little visit got me into all this trouble."

"Well, what *did* happen?" Hila's curiosity now had no bounds. She was insisting that Enela tell all in the best girl-to-girl fashion. Enela finally gave in and told Hila about her afternoon on the cliff above the dig. She included a description of the door and the back room, but she played down her fascination with Mary. Enela didn't think that would go over so well. When she had finished, Hila just sat there and stared at her.

"You can close your mouth now", Enela joked.

"Are you sure about that door you went through?" Hila looked quite serious.

"Yes, positive," Enela answered. "Of course, once it shut it was pitch black in there, so I didn't have a chance to see what, if anything, was in the room. I would really like to go back and check out that room!" As soon as she said that last sentence, Enela regretted her words. Hila, however, was deep in thought.

She's remembering something, Enela thought to herself.

"You know, I would, too," Hila even surprised herself. "I studied something about the early residents around here. I can't seem to remember them having the mechanical sophistication to create anything like what you described. I would really like to examine that room."

"I suppose we could do that. I mean, if you really want to…" Enela tried her best to sound nonchalant. Her heart was pounding in her ears like a sledgehammer. She waited for Hila's response … and waited … and waited …

Hila took her time in answering. She had never dreamed of violating the rules so blatantly. What would Ari-Ana say if she not only let Enela leave the Valley again without permission, but also went with her? Yet, the thought of being able to examine that strange doorway was so attractive … Perhaps Ari-Ana wouldn't be so observant now that she was supposed to be responsible for Enela. And she had been quite busy of late on some project or other. Maybe if they only went out for an hour or so? Late in the day? … No, it was against the rules, and she had promised to keep Enela in the Valley. She had given her word.

"What if you went out first?" Enela offered. "Then you wouldn't be here to keep me from going out … " It was a very weak argument, but it was all Enela could think of at the moment.

"We just can't, Enela," Hila appeared resigned to following the rules. "Ari-Ana would be furious!"

"Okay," Enela challenged, "then you tell me where that doorway came from and what's hiding behind it." Enela not only wanted to check out the door, she hoped to see Mary again, if only briefly. She decided this was her only chance to press her case.

"Even if I did agree," Hila offered, "how could we ever manage it?"

"Tomorrow, afternoon," Enela had been thinking about doing just this very thing for some time. "Everyone will be settled into afternoon chores and no one will need anything from the supply bunker. We can make our way to the entrance and duck over to the pueblo butte for an hour or so and still be back in time to check in the supplies."

"What if someone finds us missing … ?" Hila wasn't quite convinced.

"I'll simply say that I had to go piss and you went with me," Enela suggested. "Maybe we took the long way around, or just went for a walk. There is no rule that says I have to stay in the bunker all the time. I could even be attending to my duty of maintaining the pits. Piece of cake!"

"Let me think about it," Hila said.

"Hey," Enela just had another thought. "You aren't going to report this little discussion to Ari-Ana, are you?"

"No," Hila said. "Ari-Ana didn't tell me to report on what you are thinking about. Just to stay with you at all times and make sure you don't leave the Valley." Hila changed the subject and the two spent the rest of the evening watching the sky darken and the stars come out over the Valley.

Chapter 5

Exploring the Cave

The next morning Enela was up early and was already busy at the supply bunker when Hila showed up. "You know I'm supposed to stay with you," Hila chided as she joined in to prepare for the daily routine.

"Don't worry," Enela joked. "I haven't left the Valley without you … yet."

Now that the supplies were properly organized, there was much less work to do and the two were soon just sitting around waiting for the other Elders to stop by to check out their tools for the day.

"You know," Enela ventured, "I don't have another session with Red Hawk until tomorrow. We are going to have a lot of free time today. How shall we spend it? I don't feel like just sitting around here all day."

"I know what you're getting at," Hila said. "You want to go back to the pueblo again. I can't let you do that!"

"Admit it," Enela persisted. "You know you want to investigate that door mechanism. We could be out of here in an hour or so and be back right about lunchtime. No one would ever notice that we were gone. Now that you are supposed to be covering my tail, I'll bet that Ari-Ana isn't even monitoring me that closely."

"That's right!" Hila came back. "Ari-Ana is depending on me. I'm not going to let her down.

Even if I do want to see that door, I'm not going to leave the Valley without permission … and you aren't either!"

"Okay, Hila, I give in." Enela conceded. "I guess I'll just spend the day checking the toilets. Want to help with that, too?"

"Sure, why not?" Hila was a bit surprised at how easily Enela had capitulated, but why look a gift horse in the mouth…

"I'm going to start with the ones in the north end of the Valley, and then work my way to the south. I'll take the ones on the west side; you can tend to those on the east side." With that the two started out toward the north end of the Valley. After a bit Enela turned off to the west. Hila continued on toward the northeast. Then she stopped abruptly. Enela had been carrying a tote bag. Why did she need a tote bag? Could Enela have duped her that easily? Hila took off at a fast run toward the toilet that Enela was supposed to be checking. She wasn't there! Hila quickly turned to the south and ran on. At the next toilet she found Enela just adding a light covering of new sand to the bottom of the pit.

"What are you doing here?" Enela asked. "I thought you were doing the ones on the east side of the Valley. Oh! I get it! You thought I was running out on you. Don't you trust me?"

If an Elder could actually blush, Hila would have been a bright red at this point. She made a lame apology, asked Enela to forgive her mistrust, and headed quickly back to the northeast end of the Valley, forgetting completely about the tote bag.

Enela finished renewing the toilet, then paused to empty her bladder. Making sure that Hila was out of sight, Enela turned south and made a beeline for the exit cave. As she neared the cave entrance she stopped long enough to be sure that no one was around to see her leave the Valley. Then she ducked into the cave and bumped into …

"Hila! What are you doing here?" Enela was totally shocked.

"Just doing my job," Hila answered.

"But, how…?"

"No big thing. I didn't really go back north; I just ducked into the shadows behind a tree. When I saw you looking around suspiciously, I knew exactly what you had in mind. I didn't have to worry about anyone seeing me, so I could get here directly. Ta-da!" Hila waved her arms to emphasize her victory. "Now, shall we go back to the Valley?" Hila turned and gestured as she spoke. She was no longer blocking the entire passage. Enela darted around her and continued through the passage to the outside entrance.

"You think you're so fast, catch me – if you can!" Enela taunted gently as she ran on. Hila was surprised by the sudden move, but immediately gave chase. Enela was not as muscular as Hila, but she was speedier when running flat out. Hila did not catch up until Enela had finally stopped at the rear of the pueblo butte.

"Now that we're here, why don't we go up and check out that trick door?" Enela asked when Hila came up, panting slightly. Hila was as mad as a wet cat at having been tricked, but Enela was smiling with an impish grin and Hila gave up and started chuckling. "Well, as long as we are here …" she agreed.

It took only a few minutes for the two to climb up the rocks until they were even with the first ledge. As they made their way around to the west side of the butte, they heard voices coming from the ground below. Enela and Hila dropped down out of sight and peered over the ledge warily.

"But, Professor, you have to give us another chance. You aren't being fair…" the voice belonged to the student who had been called 'Brian'.

"Fair!" It was Professor Gauss. "You know nothing about fairness! I have already turned in the grades and the two of you flunked the course. It is as simple as that."

"We did the best we could!" another student interjected. "We just couldn't find anything of value in the plots you assigned us."

"You just didn't apply yourselves," the professor was direct and accusatory. "That was the problem. Between the two of you, you catalogued less than half the material than any of the other students. Randy and Betty came back after the class finished and helped me remove the remaining artifacts from your plot. If you had devoted as much time to this class as you apparently devote to sports, you might even have passed. Now this conversation is over. I have work to do." With that the Professor dismissed the students who grudgingly walked back to their car.

"Hi, Enela! Who's that with you?" Enela and Hila had been so wrapped up in the scene below they had not heard Mary approaching from the far end of the ledge. Enela was startled, Hila was frozen and in desperate fear for her life.

"Oh, hi, Mary," Enela offered. "Hila, this is my friend, Mary. The one I told you about …"

"Gila? As in Gila Monster?" Mary was quite proud of her contribution.

"I am not a monster!" Hila retorted, quite put out by the imagined insinuation.

"I'm sorry," Mary apologized quite contritely. "I was just making a joke. I thought your name sounded like that of a common desert lizard."

"I'm not a lizard, either!" Hila was becoming defiant.

"Oh, Enela, help me!" Mary was trying to undo any damage she had caused, but Enela was laughing too hard to be of any immediate help to anyone. Hila was watching the other two and slowly broke down and chuckled at her own reaction.

"Hila is my, uh, sister" Enela finally managed to say. That would explain their resemblance, she thought. "I brought her up here to see that curious little door you showed me. She's interested in mechanical things."

"I'm interested in all sorts of things," Hila chimed in. "The 'Professor', is he your father, Mary?" Mary nodded. "Is he always so … so … disagreeable?" Hila had another word in mind, but she was trying to be kind.

"He's really a pretty nice guy," Mary wasn't too quick to defend him. "But he has this little hang-ups. It seems to have gotten worse since my mother died. He doesn't tolerate Jews or Blacks

36

or Mexicans or Indians very well. He seems to prefer white people."

"Then he'd really like us," Enela suggested.

"Oh, no!" Mary responded. "You may be white, but you are too white, too different. He would have a fit if he knew I was up here with you."

Mary had been keeping an eye on her father down below. He was beginning to pack up some of his equipment. "I'm not going to have time to show you the door. Do you remember how it works, Enela?"

"Yes," Enela answered. "I think I can figure it out."

Just then Professor Gauss called out from below, "Mary where are you? I have to get back to my afternoon class. I'll have to finish here tomorrow."

"I'm up here on the ledge," Mary answered him. "I'll be right down." She turned back to Enela. "I may not be able to get back out here for a while. Do you have a phone number?"

"No, I don't have a phone," Enela said sadly, then she added, "But I could call you, if I had your number." Mary pulled out a piece of paper and hastily scribbled down her number. "It's better to call in the evening, and, if my father answers, tell him you're 'Linda' and you are a friend of mine from school." She thrust the paper to Enela's hand as "Mary!" came up from down below.

"I'm coming, Daddy!" She shouted and raced down the ledge to the ladder at the far end.

When she got to the bottom where her father was waiting she found him gazing up at the ledge.

"What were you doing up there?" he asked.

"Just poking around," Mary said cautiously.

"Was anyone up there with you?" Professor Gauss was still staring up at the ledge. Mary followed his gaze, but could see nothing out of the ordinary.

"No, I was alone," she answered. "I thought you wanted to leave … "

"Um, yes," her father was still interested in the ledge. "Some of the students have been saying that this pueblo is haunted. They report seeing ghosts." He slowly turned back to his car and he and Mary headed back to Winton.

Once Mary and her father had left the area, Enela led Hila to the room that housed the mysterious door. Even at noon, the room was dark. Hila was not surprised when Enela pulled two large flashlights out of the tote bag she had been schlepping.

"You had this all planned out," Hila accused Enela. The latter just grinned back. "Watch this," she said. Enela went to the back wall of the room and felt around the floor with her feet until she found the hidden pedals. As Hila watched, the wall elevated slightly and split in two. One portion swung forward and the other swung toward the rear. She took the flashlight that Enela offered and moved up to the wall to examine this new marvel. "No pueblo Indian ever designed this!" was all that she could say.

While Hila was examining the door, Enela went beyond the door to examine the room behind it. The last time she was there it was too dark for her to see anything. Now, even with the flashlight, it was hard too see much. The room was bare. There was no furniture, no fire ring. There was a large urn sitting in the back right corner. Its round bottom seemed to be sitting in an indentation in the floor, which kept it from falling over. Enela kept looking around, searching for some indication of what the room was all about. If the Indians didn't build it, then who did, and why.

Hila was engrossed in the doors. They were counterbalanced perfectly and designed to swing open when they were raised out of the channel they sat in. When they were closed they settled back into the channel and fitted with such exact nicety that there was no apparent gap between them. The levers that were fitted into the floor on the inside and outside of the doors, when moved in concert, would lift the doors and allow them to open. The configuration was simple, but certainly not known to the original inhabitants of the pueblo. She nearly died of fright when she heard Enela scream.

"Hila – Hila, look at this!"

Hila came into the room to see Enela staring at the back wall. She looked like she was in a state of shock. Hila tried to see what Enela was looking at, but the back wall was still obscured in the dim light. She brought her flashlight to bear and added her light to Enela's. She carefully walked closer, not quite sure what the excitement was all about.

"What is it, Enela?" She asked.

"Look over here," Enela said and directed her light to the right side of the wall.

Hila followed with her light and peered into the darkness. "I don't see... oh, those marks?"

"Yes, those marks!" Enela exclaimed. "Look at them closely. What do you see?"

Hila peered at the markings. They were almost indistinct. They certainly weren't cave paintings; they didn't even look like anything rational, just some scratches on the wall. But the more she looked, the more obvious it became. There were nine more-or-less round indentations of varying sizes strung out across the right side of the wall. Lines connected eight of them to a larger one. There were two other lines emanating from each of the smaller holes. Hila paused to search her memory for something similar. Slowly one object materialized. It wasn't quite the same, but it was close enough. "That's our solar system, minus Pluto. Now I know this was not designed by any early inhabitant of this area."

"That's not all", Enela was sounding truly excited. "Now look over here." She directed her light to the left side of the wall. Hila now knew what to look for and it took no time for her to make out some other scratches on that side of the wall. Again there were different sized indentations with lines connecting them, but they didn't fit any pattern that she recognized. Even searching her memory brought out no useful information.

"So what is it?" Hila asked.

"I'm guessing that it is another star system," Enela answered cautiously. "Like ours, only different."

"How can that be?" Hila was incredulous. "Are you trying to tell me that we are not the only aliens who have visited this planet? Or is this something you have dreamed up just as a joke?" Hila was not really convinced now that the markings were anything but modern made-up scratches.

Enela was indignant, "Hila, we are the only aliens on this planet! And I have never been in this room but once before. Mary can attest to that, she put me here to hide me. I didn't have any light, and I was only here for a few minutes. Maybe these marks were made by our ancestors!"

"Maybe Mary made the marks," Hila was not convinced, "or some other human made them."

"That's always possible," Enela agreed. "But maybe we should let the Councilors make that decision. You know they are always searching for some hint as to our history."

"You aren't thinking about telling Ari-Ana that we came here!" Hila had visions of being executed in the middle of the Council chamber.

"I sure am!" Enela enthused. "And I think we ought to take this urn back with us, too." Enela moved over to the urn and prepared to heft it out of its place. However, it was not nearly as heavy as it looked and came away with such ease that Enela stumbled backward. At the same time a piece of the floor came loose and fell into the indentation that had been holding the urn. For a second there was no sound, then a strange 'clink' echoed through the room.

Chapter 6

Into the Abyss

Enela set the urn down carefully and went to investigate its original resting place. There, where the urn had been resting, appeared to be a hole in the floor. The flashlights were not strong enough to show the bottom. But they did provide enough light for Enela and Hila to see that the sides of the hole were quite smooth. "Man made," were the only words Enela could come up with.

"Let's try another piece of stone," Hila suggested. Enela broke off another piece of stone and dropped it into the hole. Again a second passed before the stone landed with a satisfying 'thunk'.

"That's not the same sound," Enela complained. "I'm going to try again." She broke off a third piece of stone from the edge of the hole and dropped in on the far side. After yet another second, a 'clink' echoed back.

"There is definitely something down there!" Enela exclaimed. The two peered intently down the hole with their flashlights, but the lights still weren't powerful enough to reach the bottom. Hila, having satisfied her curiosity about the door, was more than ready to return to the Valley. Enela paced in silence, deep in thought. As she paced, she wandered out to the bright sunlight of the ledge.

"That's it!" she exclaimed, drawing Hila out to the ledge beside her.

"What's it?" Hila asked, looking down at the dig area. But Enela was already running down the ledge toward the ladder. Hila joined Enela on the ground where the latter was examining a large spool of cord that Professor Gauss had left behind.

"Oh, no!" Hila groaned. "It will never support you, even assuming that you could fit in the hole. And we have no way to anchor it." Enela ignored her plaints. She was too busy testing the strength of the cord and looking up at the ledge.

"It will support me as long as it doesn't fray," Enela assured Hila. "And I will fit in that hole. Come on and bring that rake with you." Enela headed back to the ladder carrying the spool of cord with her. Once they returned to the back room, Enela laid out her plan. She would tie the cord around her waist and drop into the hole. Hila would sit at the edge of the hole, place the rake handle across the hole and run the cord over the rake handle. The smooth handle would keep the cord from fraying and make it a little easier for Hila to manage the weight. "After all," Enela concluded, "you might as well put all that muscle to some good use." She ignored Hila's pleas for the application of some common sense.

When Enela had the cord secured about her waist, she went over to the hole and eased herself into it. It was a snug fit, but she was sure she could make it – as long as the shaft remained a constant size all the way down and had smooth sides. Hila sat down at the edge of the hole, placed the rake across it and braced it against her feet. Then she started slowly letting out the cord.

Enela had secured her flashlight to the cord about her waist and let it hang down so that it would illuminate the area below her. It did no good. There was nothing but blackness below. The smooth sameness of the sides made it very difficult for Enela to judge how far she had dropped. She called up to Hila every so often, more for reassurance than anything else.

Just as Hila cautioned her that there was only some ten feet of useful cord remaining, Enela's feet suddenly swung freely, no longer bound by the sides of the shaft. She called back to Hila to let out as much cord as she could. As Enela dropped out of the shaft she could feel the coolness of the chamber she had just entered. A minute later her feet landed on a solid surface.

"I'm at the bottom!" Enela shouted back up to Hila.

Enela took a few seconds to get her balance. She was on a flat surface, at something of an angle. But the flashlight was still of no help. She checked it to make sure it was working. It was. And it clearly illuminated her when she pointed it at herself. But when she pointed at the ground, there was nothing but blackness. She reached down and touched the surface. It was smooth and hard. Slowly she started to move up the slope. In a few steps she banged her head against the top of the cave. So, she turned around and moved down the slope.

Hila had let the cord go slack after Enela had announced her arrival at the bottom, but was still holding on to it. Indeed, she had taken the time to wrap it around the rake handle. "Just in case," Hila thought to herself.

Suddenly there was a shriek from down below at the cord almost leaped out of Hila's hands. She grabbed it and pulled it tight around the rake handle. Then she yelled down to Enela. Dead silence. "Hila could feel Enela's weight on the cord, which appeared to be swinging freely. Then it dawned on her that she could not pull Enela back up into the shaft without her cooperation. Panic began to set in.

"Enela!" Hila screamed down the hole. "Are you all right?" There was still no response.

As for Enela, she had been slowly moving down the surface she was on. She was still unable to see whatever it was she was standing on. Then, without warning, she stepped off into thin air. She automatically cried out at the surprise, then Hila grabbed the cord and Enela came to an abrupt stop in mid air. The jerk of the cord had rendered her breathless. It took almost a minute for her to get her wits about her. Enela grabbed the cord and righted herself. Then she called up to Hila to let her know she was all right.

Enela used her flashlight to look around. It seemed to be working better now. She could make out a dark shadow just above her. Her cord was draped over the edge of it. Off to the side she thought she saw some large rocks. But, best of all, just below her feet, maybe three feet further down, appeared to be the floor of the cave. Enela called up to Hila to let her down some more. Slowly she dropped the few feet to the floor of the cave.

When Enela reached the floor of the cave, she yelled back up to Hila,

"I'm on the ground. Tie off the end of the rope I'm going to untie my end so I can explore more easily."

"Be careful!" faintly came down from above.

After Enela released her end of the rope, she paused to look over her surroundings. Now the flashlight did show the floor quite clearly. Enela began to explore. The walls she could see were plain stone, just as smooth as the shaft had been. There was something large in the middle of the cave, almost filling it. But it appeared to be in shadows; the flashlight would not illuminate it properly, no matter how close she got to it. On one side were many loose rocks and a few boulders. Enela deduced that was the side that had collapsed.

As Enela looked up at the rocks a spark of light caught her attention. The more she looked at it, the more curious it became. Without even considering the danger of loose rocks, Enela started to climb up toward the light. It was difficult climbing and holding the flashlight at the same time; but she had to have some source of light to examine the rocks for the best path up.

When she neared the light, it seemed to disappear. She had to drop back a bit to relocate it. She noted its location and climbed back up to it. The mysterious light was coming in from the outside through a small gap between two rocks. Enela clung to the rock wall while she found a smaller rock she could use to enlarge the opening. By the time she was finished she had made a fairly large opening in the rocks – at least large enough for her to squeeze out of. But that was for later. Now that the cave was illuminated from the outside, she turned off the flashlight and returned to her examination of what it contained.

Despite the extra light, the cave still seemed darker than she expected. Although, it was brighter than the flashlight had been able to make it. Enela could now make out what was sitting in the middle of the cave. It was circular, about 50 feet in diameter, and convex at the top and bottom. It stood about 5 feet off the floor on thin legs and seemed to have a five-foot band separating the top and bottom halves. It looked just like some weirdo's vision of a flying saucer.

The more Enela looked at it, the more she became convinced that it was indeed something from out of this world. The legs appeared to be metallic. But the surface of the object was quite odd. It wasn't metallic, exactly; but it was hard and shiny. At least it gave the appearance of being shiny. But when she pointed the flashlight at the surface, it did not reflect the light. It actually seemed to absorb the light.

Enela tried a few experiments with the flashlight. It definitely gave off more light when she pointed it away from the strange object. As Enela wandered around the cave, she noticed that the closer to the ship she came the cooler she felt.

She examined as much of the lower surface as she could get light to. There was no sign of an opening, or even of a seam. No apparent windows, no markings, nothing but a clean, flat surface. Enela went back to where the cord dangled over the edge of the ship and pulled on it gently.

"Hila, are you still there?" Enela called up toward the shaft.

"Yes, I'm here," came the distant reply. "But it's getting late and we had better be getting back."

"Okay," Enela called back. "I'm going to climb up the cord a ways. Is it secure?"

"Yes," Hila reassured her, "I tied it off."

With that, Enela grabbed onto the cord and pulled herself up to the top of the ship. The top surface was just like the bottom surface. There were no marks, no seams, no openings. Enela went over to the edge and lay down so that she could peer over to look at the vertical side. She couldn't be sure, but it appeared to be made of the same 'metallic' substance. Still there were no discernible markings. There was a seam of sorts where the top and bottom halves met the center section, but Enela could not see any sign of an opening.

"Enela!" Hila was getting impatient.

"Yes! Hold on! I'm coming." Enela grabbed onto the cord.

Up above, Hila saw the cord go taut. She finally relaxed as she prepared to help Enela up out of the shaft. Then the cord went slack again. Hila leaped back to hole and peered down the shaft. Of course, she could see nothing. She yelled for Enela, but there was no answer. Panic set in. What if something had happened to Enela? There was no way she could fit into the shaft. She would have to go back to the Valley for help. Hila reached out and tested the cord. It was definitely slack. She called down the shaft, yelling Enela's name over and over again, straining to hear even the faintest response.

"Here I am!" Enela's calm response was as shocking to Hila as an icy shower. The response didn't come from the shaft, but from behind Hila.

She jumped up and spun around to see Enela standing nonchalantly at the door of the room.

"How did you get there!?" Hila was incredulous. Her emotions passed through several stages: from worry and anxiety to shock, disbelief, relief and finally anger. Enela just stood there for a few seconds, savoring the moment.

"Come on," she said at last. "I'll show you." Enela grabbed the urn; then they sealed the room, leaving the cord and the rake in place. Then Enela led Hila down to the end of the ledge and around it to the rock fall. They then climbed up over the rocks to a small opening between two large boulders. Leaving the urn outside among the rocks, Enela led the way through the hole, showing Hila where to step. Once inside the two made their way down to the bottom of the cave.

Hila was even more astonished when she got a good view of the strange object.

"This has to be some sort of a joke!" Hila was not ready to accept the object as some sort of spacecraft without a whole lot more proof, but even she had to admit that the object was quite strange.

"I don't know if it will fly or not," Enela conceded. "At least not until we figure out how to get inside. I just wanted you to see it so Ari-Ana will not think I am a raving lunatic when we tell her what we found."

"What exactly did 'we' find?" Hila's scientific bent was beginning to take control.

"Well," Enela reviewed what she had learned so far, "what ever it is, it appears to absorb energy, it has no discernable entry point and it seems to be made of some kind of material that I

49

have never even heard of: sort of a combination of metal and ceramics."

The two spent a while examining the find then exited again through the hole in the rocks and made their way back to the Valley with the urn. Before seeking out Ari-Ana they carefully placed the urn within the far reaches of the supply bunker. No sooner than they had done that, the word came that Ari-Ana was waiting for them in the Council chamber.

"Ari-Ana will have to congratulate us for this find!" Enela exulted as they made their way to the Council chamber.

"Hila, I am so disappointed in you!" Ari-Ana was in an absolute snit. "I knew that Enela was a flake, but I thought I could count on you!"

"Hila just stood there staring at the floor. She was too ashamed to even offer a response. She had never been in trouble like this before, but she was sure that Ari-Ana did not expect a response.

Enela, on the other hand was just bursting for a chance to tell Ari-Ana what they had found. She didn't wait for Ari-Ana to start in on her. As soon as she turned toward her, Enela took a deep breath and started her own tirade.

"Ari-Ana, you just have to hear what we found at the old pueblo butte!" Enela did take time to pause for a breath, she just rattled on non-stop. "I think it may have been one of the ships that brought our people to this planet. At least it appears to be some sort of a space ship! And there is a map of some strange solar system, a star chart of some sort. It may point to our origin! It's all hidden behind a secret room. Both Hila and I saw it, didn't we, Hila? You just have to come and look at it. But don't punish Hila! I tricked her into going out to the pueblo. She didn't want to. She really did try to stop me … " Enela finally ran out of breath and had to pause.

For the first time in recorded history, Ari-Ana stood there with her mouth open, totally speechless. "Wait a minute," she finally managed to get out. "What is it you are trying to tell me, Enela? Take your time and fill in the details."

Enela took a breath, but before she could start again, Ari-Ana repeated her instructions to take it slow and be thorough. Enela and Hila explained everything that had happened that afternoon, prompting each other from time to time. Ari-Ana paid close attention, even to the point of tracing Enela's thoughts as she spoke.

When she had finally absorbed the entire story, Ari-Ana had calmed down considerably. "If this isn't some sort of a fantastic hoax, you two may have stumbled on something quite remarkable. But it doesn't excuse the fact that the two of you have disobeyed big time! For the time being, go back to your usual chores. But if I ever hear of either of you leaving the Valley without permission again, so help me I will banish both of you! Permanently! Do you understand?"

Both Enela and Hila nodded quite abashedly.

"Then you are dismissed … " Ari-Ana said. "No, wait a minute!" she exclaimed. "Enela, just who is this 'Professor Gauss'? Have you met him?"

"He is Mary's father," Enela explained. "He teaches at the Winton College. He is the one who set up the 'dig'. I have overheard him talk with his students, but I never actually met him. I think he has some sort of a problem with humans who aren't like him. But Mary is quite nice!"

"I take it then that you have talked with Mary?" Ari-Ana was beginning to get too personal for Enela's liking.

"Yes", Enela answered, "she surprised me once when I was on the ledge," Enela did her very best to keep her mind closed on this subject. "I told her I lived out in the desert somewhere. Then she caught Hila and me together today. I told her we were sisters."

Ari-Ana digested this information for a minute or two, then sent Enela and Hila on their way. Ari-Ana had the strangest feeling that trouble was brewing, but she couldn't put her finger on the exact problem.

Ari-Ana spent the next two hours retracing Enela's steps through the pueblo. The back wall of the secret room was too rough to permit her to make a tracing of the images scratched into it, so she just made an exact mental image and tucked it away for future reference. When she was through in the room, she rewound the cord and returned it and the rake to the ground at the base of the pueblo. Then she climbed into the cave to inspect the 'strange object'. By the time she left she was satisfied that it was no hoax.

Chapter 7

What's This?

When Ari-Ana had dismissed them, Enela and Hila went back to the supply bunker. Hila was absolutely no company. She was still infuriated that she had let herself be tricked into disobeying Ari-Ana and leaving the Valley. She could still foresee Ari-Ana invoking some horrible punishment on her for her part in the crime. Enela, on the other hand, was quite sure that they had escaped unscathed. Her nonchalance just made Hila even more worried. But the afternoon and evening passed without any further word from Ari-Ana. Eventually, even Hila began to relent, a little bit. It wasn't until they were relaxing after supper that Hila suddenly spoke out.

"Wait a minute!" Hila suddenly exclaimed, "We didn't tell Ari-Ana about the urn we found!"

"I know," Enela answered. "I did my best not to think about it. It may be nothing, but I have the sneaking suspicion that it has something to do with that thing over there in the cave. It was just too conveniently placed. That's my ace in the hole."

"What do you mean?" Hila was getting worried again. "We should have told Ari-Ana about it. She's going to get mad at us again!"

"I'll tell her about it," Enela did her best to reassure Hila. "But first I want to take a look inside it. I was just waiting for things to die down a bit so I wouldn't be interrupted".

"But it's sealed," Hila tried to protest. Enela just ignored her and started poking around among the strange artifacts stored in the back of the bunker. In a few minutes she came back with the urn, an old coffee can and a propane torch.

"It looks like it is sealed with wax or pitch," Enela said, digging at the substance with her fingertips. "I'll bet that this torch will melt whatever it is and free the stopper."

With that, Enela sat down and started heating the mouth of the urn, carefully holding it over the can. In a few minutes a substance started dripping down into the can. A few more minutes and Enela was able to pry the lid out. She turned off the torch and waited for the clay urn to cool.

As soon as it was relatively safe, Enela carefully tipped up the urn and shook it. There was a little rattle, but nothing came out. Enela was about to reach down into the urn with her hand, but Hila grabbed her arm and just shook her head. Enela stopped to consider her act for a minute, then she grabbed the big screwdriver she had used to pry out the top and plunged it down into the urn. Nothing happened. She moved it around a bit. Still nothing.

Enela pulled the screwdriver out and examined it. It was dry and clean. No liquid, no dust. She looked at Hila, then shrugged and put her hand slowly down into the urn. She felt around, stopped and slowly withdrew her hand. She was holding what appeared to be a sheaf of papers. Enela put the papers down, picked up the jug, inverted it and shook it. There was no sound, no nothing.

Hila and Enela put the urn and the other items to one side and looked at the papers that were lying between them. The pages weren't really paper, but they served the same purpose. They contained what appeared to be writing. But the characters were of no alphabet either of them had ever seen.

To be sure, Enela went back to the library section and brought out a reference book on various alphabets. There was nothing even close. Each character was made up of a black square with parts, or pieces, missing. Some angles were curved, some straight. The characters were divided into varying sized groups with space between them. Enela suggested that the groups probably sufficed for words or thoughts.

The two studied the pages for some time. They turned them in various directions. Enela even tried to turn them over and read them from behind, but the pages were opaque. Hila thought of using a mirror, but that didn't yield anything useful. Finally, Hila had had enough.

"I give up," she said. "I'm tired and I'm going to get some sleep. You aren't planning on going back out to the pueblo butte, are you?"

"No," Enela answered. "I've had my fill of that butte for one day. I just want to study these a little while longer, then I am going to turn in, too. I'll see you here tomorrow morning."

Hila wandered off to her sleeping quarters and Enela bent back over the pages once again. She lost all track of time as she sat there and pondered the strange markings. Then slowly she began to understand. A word here, then a word there. She didn't even realize what was happening until she came across a complete sentence, which she somehow understood.

"To open the entry – place your hand on the symbol … "

Enela had been in a sort of trance, but this realization brought her quickly back to the present. She looked at the passage she had just 'read'. The characters stared dumbly back at her, just as incomprehensible as they had ever been. Enela shook her head to clear out the cobwebs. Had she just 'read' that line or had she dreamed it? Maybe she was so tired that she wasn't thinking clearly. Maybe she was hallucinating.

She looked at the line again, logically this time. Most of the two- and three-letter groupings ended with the same character. If that was the 'ee' sound; and that other tailing letter was an 'ah' sound … It couldn't be that simple! Then an even greater, more astounding thought occurred. Enela stopped abruptly. She had to find out if she was right.

Enela took a couple of deep breaths and cleared her mind. She tried desperately to quell the excitement that was growing within her. She let her mind go blank, picked up another page and focused on the writing. Slowly she plumbed the depths of her memory, deeper and deeper, to places she had never been before. Then, little by little, the characters became words and the words formed sentences, concepts, instructions.

Without losing her focus, Enela picked up another page and continued. Several pages contained words Enela had never seen or heard, there were pages of mostly numbers that she didn't understand at all. But the rest of it was becoming clear. The pages were written in Eldertongue, the Elder language! Even stranger, the words, the grammar, the usage was familiar! It was the same language that the Elders in the Valley spoke among themselves. But with the race memory, there had been no need for a written language. Everyone was born with a complete record of Elder history from the time they arrived on this planet. Before that, there were no records of any kind, written or otherwise.

Enela was stunned. Where had this come from? More important, *when* had it come from. Was all of this just some gigantic hoax? Had Ari-Ana set this up just as another object lesson. Was Ari-Ana back at the Council chamber laughing her head off at the 'space ship' that Enela and Hila had found? There were just too many questions and Enela was just too tired to struggle with them any longer. She rolled up the pages and stowed them back in the urn. Then she put the stopper back in the urn and stowed it securely in a back corner of the supply bunker.

She would think about this again tomorrow. No, it already was tomorrow by the clock on the shelf. Enela went over to the dry goods section, found a soft spot and lay down. She was asleep before she had time to get comfortable.

The next morning it seemed as though everyone in the Valley needed something from the supply bunker. Enela and Hila had no time to give a thought to the strange pages, which had been in the urn. By midmorning, just as things were beginning to quiet down, a message arrived from Ari-Ana. She wanted to see Hila at once in the Council chamber.

Hila gave Enela a quizzical look. "I guess this is where I get the axe," she said somewhat hesitatingly.

"Am I supposed to come, too?" Enela asked Hila.

"No," she replied. "Ari-Ana only sent for me."

Enela was in a bit of a quandary. "Well, what am I supposed to do?" she asked no one in particular.

"Well, when you're finished here I guess you could make the rounds of the toilets … " Hila was trying to be funny, but the joke fell flat. Enela didn't know whether to throw something at her or tell her off; so she just stood there glaring. Hila got the hint and hurried off.

Enela worked off her anger by cleaning up the bunker. In the process she again began to think about the mysterious pages. She decided to study them some more. She reviewed the page that told how to gain access to the space ship. It was the easiest to read and she had soon memorized it. Then she put the pages back and left the bunker. She was worried about Hila. After all, it was Hila who wanted to do the right thing. She didn't deserve to be severely punished just because Enela had managed to trick her into leaving the Valley. Enela decided that she would go over to the Council chamber and try to intercede for Hila.

On the way to the Council chamber Enela glanced at the shadows to determine what time it was. "Early afternoon," she guessed. That meant that Hila had been gone over three hours. That long, and no word yet – Enela picked up the pace.

When she got to the Council chamber she hurried in, expecting to find Ari-Ana engrossed in some task. Instead, she – almost literally – bumped into …

" Ari-Ula! Oh, please excuse me!" Enela quickly backed up a pace and bowed to the Chief Councilor. "I am sorry to disturb you. I was looking for Ari-Ana. Is she available?"

"No," Ari-Ula replied. "She went out to the pueblo butte this morning with Hila and Arina. I don't know when she will return."

Enela was in a state of shock. Why had Ari-Ana taken Hila and Arina to the pueblo? More importantly, why had Ari-Ana not included her?

"Enela, Enela!" Ari-Ula was doing her best to break through. Finally, Enela came back to the present.

"I'm sorry, Ari-Ula. You were saying … ?"

"I was saying that Red Hawk has already arrived and is waiting for you in the side chamber." Ari-Ula was looking curiously at Enela. She knew that Enela was some sort of a special case, but this was the most un-Elder like person that she had ever met. Having delivered her message she turned and resumed her previous activities. She left Enela to make her way to the room where Red Hawk was waiting.

When Enela entered the room she found Red Hawk sitting there meditating. Red Hawk was wearing her trademark fine buckskin dress, open on both sides from shoulder to knee and tied loosely about the waist. It had a minimum of decoration, which Enela didn't fully understand, she simply accepted it as pretty. Enela sat down on the floor opposite Red Hawk and waited patiently for her to begin the session.

Red Hawk did not move for several minutes and Enela spent the time trying to calm her mind in preparation for their session. She was focusing so intently that she almost jumped when Red Hawk spoke,

"You seem to have something troubling you ... "

"Why ... ? I mean ... I ... Well, I ... " Enela wasn't exactly sure where to go with this.

"Suppose you just tell me what's bothering you," Red Hawk's words were uttered quite calmly. They were not a command, but they were not to be ignored, either. This was only one of the traits which Red Hawk and Ari-Ana had in common. Enela felt compelled to answer. She explained how she was feeling after Ari-Ana had selected Hila and Arina to work on the space ship and had deliberately excluded her. Red Hawk listened in silence until Enela had run out of words and feelings and finally quit speaking.

Enela had poured out all of her emotions, her anger, her elation at having found the ship, her frustration, her guilt at having disobeyed Ari-Ana. The confession was draining. At last, Red Hawk spoke.

"I am glad to see that you have assimilated your Elder heritage."

"What?" Enela was never quite sure how to interpret Red Hawk's off the wall comments.

"Not once did you indulge in the common human practice of blaming someone or something else for your problems," Red Hawk was almost beaming.

"I still don't understand," Enela complained.

"You lived among the humans for some ten years," Red Hawk explained. "Did you not ever notice how they always tend to blame others for their own shortcomings? I see it every day in my practice. It is a very hard tendency to resolve."

"Oh," Enela was pondering the question. "Yes, I see what you are saying. I never really thought about it. Sometimes the kids in our neighborhood would do bad things. If they were found out they would either lie about it or try to blame it on someone else. It was almost automatic. Why do humans act that way? Why can't they just accept responsibility for their actions?"

"Some counselors feel that it is an inherent condition," Red Hawk answered, "but I have another theory. Tell me, Enela do you believe in a god?"

The question surprised Enela. She had to stop and think about her answer. She was even more surprised at her answer…

"No, not really. I remember my human mother telling me that she had taken me to a church to have me baptized. At first she made me go to church with her almost every week. When my human father was in town he would sometimes come with us. Then when I was older I was supposed to go to the church to take classes in the form of religion they practiced. I ran away before I was supposed to be … " Enela searched for the correct word, "confirmed.

"Some of the kids I knew went to our church, some went to other churches, some didn't go to a church. But if you asked them they all would have said that they believed in 'god'. I probably would have agreed with them; it was the thing to do, it was part of their culture."

"Just so," Enela perceived that Red Hawk had moved into her teaching mode. "Most humans admit to a belief in a 'god' or gods. It is indeed part of the human culture. Some of the gods are similar in nature; some are remarkably different. Some are ephemeral; others are represented by idols. Some are all-powerful, all-knowing and present everywhere. Others have more human frailties. Some gods are angry and vengeful; some are kind and indulgent; some can be either depending on the situation. In any case every human firmly believes that his or her god is the only true god and that all other gods are false and without merit.

"Imagine, if you will, what is was like when the human animal first acquired cognition – awareness of his surroundings. Think how afraid they must have been of severe weather phenomena, of large carnivores, even of the dark of night. These were bands of hunters. If game was plentiful they had an easy life. If game was scarce they faced starvation. How easy it would have been for some individual, who was not a proficient hunter, to earn his portion of the kill by providing a magical charm or incantation, which would ensure plentiful game. When there was plenty to eat he would be hero. If the charm didn't work, he would have to invent an excuse. Maybe require a sacrifice to appease the gods. I am sure that many of these early priests failed miserably and lost their lives in the process; but some would have succeeded. Their reputation would grow as would their god or gods and their particular belief system.

"Even a cursory look back at the human history reveals a myriad of religions which sprang up in various parts of the world. Some lasted for only a short time or were relegated to a small part of the earth. Others, especially those embraced by a powerful ruler, made quite an impact on history. The ancient Egyptians, the Greeks, the Romans, each had a potent religious system. And each system was eventually overcome by a different system with better priests or a better promise of immortality or a better explanation for natural events.

"While the European and Near East areas were developing singular, humanoid deities such as Jehovah and Jesus and Allah, the people in the Orient were developing philosophical religions such as Confucianism, the Tao and Shinto. The civil authorities eventually enforced adherence to these various religions. This gave them a permanence that some of the earlier versions lacked.

"The Catholic Church, the first prominent version of Christianity, took over all of Europe and is still strong today all over the world. Islam, which was created in the seventh century took over all of the Mid-East and has now branched out over Africa and the Orient. For centuries men fought and killed each other in support of one of these religions over the others. In the end no one religion won outright. But hundreds of thousands of lives were lost in the process and we are still fighting the same battles today on a secular level.

"One of the factors that enabled both the prevalence of religion and its viciousness is the fact that almost every religion must be accepted purely on faith. Only one religion welcomes investigation and proofs of its claims. All the rest demand that their adherents accept them on faith alone. They can not be examined or probed logically or they will immediately fall apart. So, when a person accepts any particular religion he must immediately marginalize all who believe in a different religion. Otherwise, he himself would appear less intelligent. This didn't just happen between major sects, but also within sects. Moslems killed Moslems because they didn't see eye-to-eye on religious issues. Conservative Christians had no trouble killing or persecuting other Christians that didn't accept their exact beliefs.

"What was it that made these religions so powerful that men would gladly die for them, besides the faith aspect? They promised three things: first was some sort of a reward upon death, second was absolution from sins and lastly was a god who would intercede in human life if he was asked to do so. If one prayed to one's god and the outcome was favorable, all was well and good. If the outcome was not favorable, the priest just explained that 'god', in his omniscience, had something else in mind and it wasn't the petitioner's province to know what. Or maybe the petitioner wasn't being true to his religion and needed to make more confessions or more sacrifices.

"This was the beginning of the end of human independence. If something didn't go right, it was simply that god wanted things to work out that way. Whatever happened, god was in control.

What better excuse could a person have? If any person stepped up and had the audacity to say, 'I am in charge!', he was promptly reminded that god is in charge – how dare he presume to be god! Over the centuries this persistent browbeating, supported by a common culture, resulted in the average human coming to believe that he or she was never responsible for what happened. It was god's will.

"In the United States, over the past fifty years or so, this phenomenon has evolved even further. Humans have refused to admit to any sort of responsibility. They expect the government to take care of them from cradle to grave. If they do something inherently stupid, it is never their fault. They immediately look for someone else to blame and then find a lawyer to take their case to court. This is the great gift that religion has given us."

"What of the Elder people?" Enela interjected, thinking of her experiences in the Elder Valley. "Do they embrace a religion?"

"No, Red Hawk," she said. "The Elder culture has no place for religion. Most of them consider it at best a mythology, at worst a story for children that has no basis in reality. They realize that there are things that they do not know; but they don't invent fanciful tales to explain them. They either work at figuring them out rationally or simply accept what is and wait for the knowledge to come."

Red Hawk continued, "Such fanciful tales as espoused by religions only hinder us in finding the truth. Some myths, such as Santa Claus or the Easter Bunny are fine for amusing children. Religion is far too powerful an opiate to be considered safe in any form in a rational society.

That is why I was so pleased that you had not been unduly influenced by your exposure to religion when you were living among the humans."

"Why don't the humans just get rid of the religions?" Enela thought that would be a proper action.

"Once a religion has become imbedded in the society it is very difficult to eliminate it. If everyone believes a certain thing to be true – even if it is obviously false – anyone who promotes its elimination is considered to be crazy and becomes an outcast from the society. The humans have a phrase for this situation, 'fifty million Frenchmen can't be wrong'. The humans are a social race. They would not accept becoming outcasts in what would ultimately be a losing battle.

"Consider that the Judeo-Christian Bible is full of references to Jehovah talking to humans. And this is considered to be 'god's word' and an irrefutable truth. But let any human today claim that Jehovah has spoken to him, and he is immediately deemed to be mentally ill. For it is common knowledge that humans cannot talk to god except in prayer - especially those prayers led by a priest. And the only response to those prayers comes through the actions of god, not the words of god."

"Then, if humans can not shake themselves free of the yoke of religion, what is the answer?" Enela still nursed a childish hope that everything would work out well.

Red Hawk paused, as if looking inward for an answer. "That is not for us to know at this time. We can not see into the future. Perhaps a religion, such as Buddhism, which celebrates individual responsibility and which does not include a specific deity or godhead, will eventually prevail when the adherents of the other major religions have killed each other off. Whatever it will be, it will not happen in our lifetimes. So we must be prepared to deal with religion whenever we have relations with humans."

"Now," said Red Hawk, "Let's get on with our session."

For the next two hours Red Hawk guided Enela through the various levels of her memory. She drew out long buried memories, traced Enela's relatives. Some memories led to nothing but dead ends, others blossomed forth into intricate connections involving many different people and times and places. Red Hawk took careful notes of all the important happenings.

Just as Red Hawk had finished and brought Enela back into the present and awakened her, Ari-Ana entered the room. Red Hawk immediately arose and, with a nod to Ari-Ana, left the room to return to human society.

"I was told you wanted to speak to me, Enela," Ari-Ana's voice was soothing and inquisitive. The session with Red Hawk had eliminated all of Enela's pent up anger and frustration. Enela did not doubt for a minute that Red Hawk had done that on purpose. But she was really thankful for the help.

"I have something that I wanted to tell you," Enela began. "While Hila and I were at the pueblo butte the other day, we found an urn in the hidden room and brought it back to the Valley. Last night

I opened it and found some pages inside." Enela did not mention that Hila was with her when she opened the urn. She figured that if Hila had not mentioned it, she didn't want to get her into trouble.

"And what of these pages?" Ari-Ana seemed to be truly curious.

"I think that they contain instructions for the operation of the space ship," Enela offered hesitatingly.

"Where are these strange 'pages'?" Ari-Ana asked looking about the room.

"They are back at the supply bunker," Enela replied.

"Then perhaps we should go take a look at them … " Ari-Ana suggested.

The two walked back to the supply bunker in silence. When they arrived, Enela retrieved the urn and the pages from their hiding place and brought them out to Ari-Ana. The latter looked at the strange markings and repeated Enela's earlier attempts, turning the pages in every way to try to decipher the marks. She finally gave up.

"You can read this?" Ari-Ana was very definitely suspicious.

"A little of it," Enela answered. She took the pages and riffled through them to what appeared to be page 1. This she showed to Ari-Ana and attempted to read the instructions for entering the ship. Her translation was a tad sketchy and there were some words, which she did not truly know, but she got the gist of it.

Ari-Ana was not impressed. "You really expect me to   believe this?"

"I'm sure I could do better with some more time," Enela was trying not to plead. "I have only been able to study this page for an hour or two. Perhaps if I was able to actually look at the ship as I translated, I could do better … "

"Aha!" Ari-Ana interrupted. "So that's it! Are you trying to trick me into letting you work with Hila and Arina? I don't think it's going to work."

This turn of events hadn't even occurred to Enela. She almost went into panic mode. Then she abruptly reined in her emotions and offered one last attempt.

"Suppose you give me a chance to prove that these pages are the real thing. Just 24 hours to prove that I can open the ship using these instructions. If I can, I get to work with Hila and Arina. If not I'll come back here and do whatever you want. I'll be no further trouble at all. Unless, of course, you have already accessed the ship … "

Ari-Ana thought for a moment. "No, we have not been able to find a way into the ship …. All right, I'll give you 24 hours to gain access. If these pages are truly genuine and you can indeed read them, you'll get your position on the team. But if this is a joke or a trick, you have not yet felt my wrath."

Enela gulped. She had not fully realized what she had got herself into. "Okay," she said. "I agree."

When Ari-Ana left, Enela grabbed the pages and a lantern and headed out to the pueblo butte. She climbed the rock face and slipped into the hole. Once she made her way down to the ship she tried to locate the proper location for the opening. The ship was still glowing faintly, but even with the added light from the lantern, she could see nothing. After spending much time searching the ship's exterior and referring to the instruction sheet, she still had no luck.

She went over to spot near the wall and sat down to study the pages some more. She was convinced that the clue had to be somewhere in them. By now the pages had been completely shuffled and the original order lost. "If I were doing something like this, I think I would number the pages," she thought. Enela took the pages and righted them all so that they were in the same orientation as the one she could read. Then she started scanning the pages for something that looked like a page number.

The search took quite a while. There were several false starts that weren't consistent throughout the pages. Then a set of characters in the middle of the right edge of the pages seemed to be consistent. Enela arranged the pages in the new order. What she had thought to be the first page was now page three. If that were true, then there were two pages of instructions that she had to work through before she could open the ship.

It was already late at night, but Enela had no choice. If she was to open the ship as she promised, she had to decipher the other two pages. She started in on page one.

Enela spent hours working her way through the first page. Just as she was making some progress, she kept being pestered by this insect buzzing about her head. She tried to brush it away, but it would not go. Nor could she even touch it. She took a mighty swing at it and her hand smacked against the rock wall. The sting of the impact brought her fully awake.

She had been asleep. The pesky insect was only dust suspended in a shaft of the sunlight peering through the hole in the rock wall. Enela didn't know how long she had been asleep, or how much of her 24 hours she had left. She quickly picked up the pages she had dropped. Page one hadn't been much help, so she started on page two. It was shorter; surely she could translate at least part of it.

Enela let her mind wander over the page, searching for some hint as to what it said. She absently remembered the story of a girl who had been studying Greek. On her final exam she was faced with translating a passage she had never seen before. When she first looked at the text she couldn't make heads or tails of it. It all looked like gibberish. Then she saw the word *και*. She knew that it meant 'and'. With just that little push she jumped in and finished the whole translation. Enela was looking for her *και*.

It didn't come quickly, but then she saw the word for light. It was modified by another word. What kind of light? The shaft of sunlight had shifted now and was shining in her eyes. She moved to get away from it. Sunlight! The rest of the page suddenly started to make sense to her. She read on, fascinated by the text. It took a few hours, but she finally finished the page. Even with this new information she knew she could never get the ship open within her allotted 24 hours. It could take much longer. She had to get to Ari-Ana and get an extension!

Ari-Ana was in the Council chamber when Enela arrived somewhat abruptly and completely out of breath. She was somewhat taken aback at Enela's appearance.

"Have you succeeded in opening the ship?" she asked somewhat suspiciously.

"No," Enela answered. "I'm going to need more time."

"We agreed on 24 hours." Ari-Ana reminded her. "Why should I agree to change that?"

"Ari-Ana, I had the pages out of order. I have translated the page that comes before the instructions for opening the ship. We must do something else before we can open it." Enela tried to sound more confident than she really was.

"Please explain," Ari-Ana was not happy.

Enela explained as calmly as she could. "The ship apparently has some internal power generators. Over time they have run down and are not working at full power. The instructions say that they must be recharged before the ship will function normally."

"And how are they to be recharged? We don't have an electric power source." Ari-Ana was still not a happy camper. Her comment verged on being sarcastic.

Enela was ready for that question. "The ship was apparently capable of recharging itself while in space. I believe it generate power from any energy source. When I was in the cave the very first time, my flashlight was not as bright when I pointed it toward the ship as when I pointed it toward the cave walls. I think it was absorbing the energy of the light radiating from the flashlight."

"That would take a lot of flashlights!" Ari-Ana didn't   sound quite as stern.

Enela was ready with her answer, "What if we enlarged the hole in the rock wall and slanted it so that the sunlight would fall on the ship? If it can maintain itself on cosmic energy, direct sunlight ought to work even better." Enela was even beginning to sound somewhat optimistic.

"All right," Ari-Ana conceded. "If this were your project, how would you proceed?"

"I would use a crew to open the rock wall sufficiently to allow all the morning sun to fall on the ship," Enela answered. "We should be able to tell shortly if it's going to work. The ship seems to have a faint glow about it even now. I'll bet that when it is fully charged it will glow quite brightly. That will probably be sufficient to make the entry portal and its controls to become visible."

"Why not just tear the wall down?" Ari-Ana asked.

Enela wasn't brilliant by any stretch, but sometimes she had just the right answer. "I once read about a system of spy satellites," she said. "I don't know if they still exist or not, nor how good they may be; but I don't think we want the humans to know what we have found. I don't think we would like their reaction!"

"You may have a very valid point," Ari-Ana conceded. "I will consult on it. Do you plan on keeping to your original 24 hour schedule?"

"I can't possibly," Enela admitted. "But I will still get it open as soon as practical after the ship has been restored to full power."

"Good enough," Ari-Ana agreed. "Let's get started."

The crew worked the rest of that day and on into the next two. It was hard work moving the rocks in such a way as to allow the light in and still prevent a casual observer from seeing the hole in the rock wall. But progress was being made. Each day the ship seemed to glow with a little more energy. And each day Enela was in the cave examining the ship and its markings. Some of the markings were actually becoming more obvious as the energy level increased. During the night she would work on the instructions for opening the entry portal. There were still some words that she did not recognize and could not guess at.

It was about a week later that Ari-Ana suggested rather strongly that they had probably gained as much power as they were going to achieve. She and Enela and Hila and Arina went to the cave so that Enela could open the ship.

Enela did not have a lot of confidence, but it was time for her to put up or shut up. The other three waited at the side of the cave while Enela approached the ship with the instruction sheet. The page did not contain any diagrams, only words to describe the various landmarks and procedures.

Enela tried to find the starting point. It was supposed to be the 'front' of the ship. But, what was the front of a circle? There were no obvious engines to indicate the rear, there was no pointed section that might be the front. Enela walked slowly around the ship. Would the front be between two of the legs or at a leg? "Wait a minute!" she thought, "If they put this ship into the cave using its own power, they would have flown it straight in."

Enela moved to the inside of the cave. The inside section was between two of the legs. So far, so good! Then she looked up at the vertical portion of the ship, between the two curved sections. Could she discern a slight difference in texture in the center portion? A window or radar device? Maybe. She moved in toward the center, following the instructions on the page. She was looking for the markings described on the page. She squinted, she stared; nothing stood out. Then as she was turning she caught sight of something. The marks were just visible at the edge of her vision. "That was what the comment about eyes had meant!" she thought.

Enela placed her hand against the mark as the instructions had said. She pressed inward slightly. Nothing. She pressed harder. There was a sound between a hiss and a hum and a thin portion of the underside of the ship moved downward just behind her and came to rest on the floor of the cave with a pleasant sounding thud. The ship was open and ready to receive visitors.

Chapter 8

The Gray Ship

When the entry way dropped down from the underside of the ship, Enela backed up with the others near the cave wall. A soft reddish glow could be seen emanating from inside the ship. The four of them just stood there in silence and looked at the ship. It was Arina who finally spoke.

"Well, I'll be," she whispered. "Why didn't we see that spot, Hila?"

"Perhaps," said Ari-Ana, "you were handicapped by not having a map." She looked at Enela somewhat curiously. "Enela, I don't know where you acquired your ability to read Eldertongue, but it has surely proven valuable. You have also shown that you are willing to work very hard to attain a goal. I may have been too hasty in my judgment of you. If you still want to work with Hila and Arina, and if they wish to have you on their project, I will permit it."

"Oh, yes!" said Hila. "She will be a great help to us."

Arina wasn't quite so exuberant. "I don't mind," she said.

"What about you, Enela?" Ari-Ana asked.

"Of course!" Enela agreed. "We'll make a great team!"

"I'm sure you will," Ari-Ana wasn't sure about it at all. But she also recognized the importance of Enela's ability to read the 'instruction manual' she had found. Any discouragement at this point could result in the loss of that crucial information. She still didn't feel that Enela was entirely trustworthy. But she felt compelled to try once more.

"Enela, I want you to work on translating that first page. The others can wait. If these instructions are to be followed in order, we may already be in trouble. I wouldn't want this thing to suddenly explode from over stimulation, or something. Hila and Arina, you are to examine the interior of the ship and see if you can work out the controls. You are *not*, however, to attempt to operate any of the controls, or to try to move it or fly it or anything of the sort. Is that understood?"

The three nodded almost absentmindedly. Their attention was still focused on the strange ship sitting in front of them.

"Also, Enela," Ari-Ana continued, "I want you to continue seeing Red Hawk on a regular basis. It is more important now than ever."

"Of course, Ari-Ana," Enela was floating on a cloud. She would have agreed to anything at this point.

"Now, it is getting late. I think we could all use a good night's sleep. I will leave it up to you to work out a schedule to thoroughly investigate this ship, but I would like frequent progress reports. Enela, do you think you can close the entry?"

"I think so," Enela said. Actually she was far from certain, but willing to give it a try. She walked back to the area behind the ramp and carefully examined the area that had contained the open switch. She could see nothing but the one switch, so she tried it once again. Nothing happened. She again scanned the area, looking for even a jot that might indicate another switch. Nothing was visible; the skin of the ship was smooth and unblemished. In frustration Enela turned around and took a swat at the underside of the ramp. With a low hum the ramp swung up and seamlessly blended in with the underside of the ship. Surprised, but feeling proud of her accomplishment, Enela called Hila and Arina over and showed them the location of the switch. Each of them had a go at opening the ramp and then closing it again.

The four then made their way back to the Valley. Hila and Arina spent a very restless night, tossing and turning, in anticipation of the strange new things the morrow would bring.

Before turning in for the night, Enela stopped by the supply bunker where she picked up a cell phone and made her way back outside the bunker. She selected a secluded spot beside the bunker where she would be hidden by several trees. Enela recalled the number that Mary had given her and dialed the phone. She listened as the other end rang …

"Hello?" It was Professor Gauss.

"Hello," Enela said. "This is … Linda … May I speak to Mary?" Somehow Enela didn't think the Professor would appreciate her real name. She could only hope that Mary would catch on and not give everything away.

"One moment," the Professor said. Enela could hear him calling Mary and saying that it was Linda on the phone. Mary hesitated for a moment, then took the phone. Her 'hello' was hesitant.

"Mary, it's me, Enela. I thought your father might like the name 'Linda' better."

"Oh, yes," Mary responded. "How wonderful of you to call! We haven't had a chance to talk in a long time." She shooed her father away and settled down to have a nice long chat with Enela.

The two talked for over an hour. It was just 'girl talk', but Enela enjoyed it immensely. It was the perfect end to a wonderful day. Before it was over Enela had suggested that Mary get a cell phone, so that they could talk without having to bother the Professor. They also agreed that Enela would call back in three days at the same time. Before she put the phone back, Enela took the precaution of erasing the phone's log.

Enela slept soundly that night thoroughly enjoying dreams of great accolades from all in the Valley for her part in finding and opening the ship. For some strange reason Mary was also in the crowd applauding wildly.

Ari-Ana, on the other hand, did not sleep at all. She was troubled by the possibilities that this strange ship portended. She knew she would have to tell the Council about the find. She was worried that they might suggest that they simply close up the cave and purge the memories of all involved. That, indeed, might be the safest option. On the other hand … on the other hand …

The next day Enela was back at her post in the supply bunker. In between customers she was working on the first page, as Ari-Ana had directed. It was proving extremely difficult. There were many words that Enela simply did not know.

She had been able to make out enough words on the other two pages to interpolate the missing information. But not on the first page. The text was short and to the point. It had the look of a short instruction supported by an explanation. She could clearly make out a negative article a very emphatic negative. But she could not decipher what it was they were not supposed to do.

When the flow of customers stopped, she decided to go to Ari-Ana to see if there was anyone else in the Valley who might know something of the Elder language. She took the page with her and made her way to the Council chamber.

When Enela arrived, she was about to barge in as she usually did, but she stopped at the entrance. She could hear a conversation from inside the chamber. Then other voices arose. There was a Council meeting in progress. Enela had never been present at a Council meeting. It wasn't prohibited for members of the Valley to attend Council meetings unless they were specifically invited, but the meetings weren't usually announced unless the subject was of particular interest to a large number of Elders. Looking into the chamber, Enela saw that a drape had been drawn across the entrance. That was a sure sign that this was a private meeting. Interlopers would not be welcome.

Enela was about to turn back and return to the supply bunker when she heard Ari-Ana's voice. She was speaking about the ship. Enela slipped back into the entranceway, staying as far to the side as she could and being careful not to disturb the drape. Her curiosity had just taken over control over her common sense.

The voices were almost hushed, speaking urgently but calmly. Enela strained to hear snippets of what was being said.

"… we don't know where the thing came from. It may have nothing to do with us … "

"… we have no experience with such things. It would be too dangerous … "

"… this may be our chance to return home … "

"… we don't even know where home is. We are better off just staying here … "

"… don't know how much longer we can stay here … can't leave the Valley … the humans are too dangerous … "

The banter continued in that vein. There was clearly no agreement. Enela couldn't figure out which side was winning the debate. It was clear that none of the Councilors knew anything about the ship in the cave. That was scary. The instructions she had found were clearly written in the Elder language. Whoever wrote them knew about the ship and was an Elder. Why didn't the Councilors at least know who it might have been?

There was a sudden movement just outside the chambers – someone was coming. In her haste to get away without being seen, Enela tripped and fell – backwards through the drape and into the middle of the Council chamber. The conversation stopped abruptly and all of the Councilors stared at Enela as she lay there sprawled in the middle of the chamber.

"Enela! What are you doing here? Don't you even know the meaning of the drape?" for a Councilor, Ari-Ana was bordering on being livid.

"Oh! Please excuse me, Ari … I tripped." It was a lame excuse, but it was the truth, and Enela couldn't think up a better response at the moment.

"Yes, it certainly appears that you did," Ari-Ula was smiling, despite the interruption. "But do tell us, dear, what was so urgent."

Ari-Ana was scowling. Enela knew she had better come up with something. She took her time in standing and bowing to the assembled Councilors. Then she had a scathingly brilliant idea …

"I was studying this page of instructions regarding the ship, as Ari-Ana instructed me. It is written in *Eldertongue*." Enela emphasized that point gently. "I know some of the words but there are others that are strange to me. I was going to ask if there was anyone who might recognize the words if I read them. I saw the drape and turned to leave, but in my haste I tripped. I apologize for my clumsiness … "

The Councilors were suddenly agog.

"Instruction manual!?"

"For the ship!?"

"Written in Eldertongue!?"

"How is it that you know the Elder language?" The first comments were generally directed at Ari-Ana; but that last question was aimed specifically at Enela.

"I don't know," she answered tentatively. "But I seem to be able to read it."

"This puts a decidedly different light on the situation, "Ari-Ula said. And a number of the Councilors murmured an agreement. "Ari-Ana, why didn't you tell us about this 'instruction manual'? I for one would like to see it."

"I was hoping that we would be able to use it to learn more about the strange ship," Ari-Ana explained. "I do not think that we know enough yet to make a wise decision as to how to proceed. Perhaps, in a few weeks, when we have had the chance to examine the ship in more detail … " Was it just Enela's imagination, or did Ari-Ana seem a bit uncomfortable?

The Councilors stood in silence for a minute or two; then Ari-Ula spoke. "It is agreed that we will continue to examine the ship, but we will take no further steps until the Council has a chance to review these instructions." Then she turned again to Enela. "I can not read the Elder script, but I do know many of the words. Suppose that you read what you do not understand. Perhaps I will be able to help."

Enela glanced at Ari-Ana. Her face was wrinkled into a frown; it was obvious that she was upset. But Ari-Ula had commanded her, so Enela unrolled the page and started reading…

-*Hilare -nifane leve `o farami*

-*nifane nivoe vulami horo*

-*nivine farani lifaumi umi evimavi*

-*ho farani mareaiui naha hani malai oni*

-*iho rahilami nivureaiui imoi*

-*vine fana ho farami vina hovi umani fiaeii vinami imo hai niaviumo*

-*ho farami vineoiui avina hani huro lieveli hora mani huro*

-hivoe rahilami hai hirane ilini nilivo hi imo ai nimuro

When Enela had finished there was a hushed quiet in the chamber. Even Ari-Ana's scowl had vanished. Finally Ari-Ula spoke …

"I have never heard our language spoken so beautifully. You are truly talented, Enela. But now let us all get down to work and figure out just what it is saying. Enela, what have you come up with so far?"

Enela explained what she understood of the passage, but there were several gaps where she did not recognize a word or a particle. All of the councilors offered advice or recollections, but it was hard work and progress was slow in coming.

While Enela was conferring with the Council, Hila and Arina were in the cave examining the strange ship. They had managed to lower the entrance ramp without much difficulty. Arina was all for entering the ship and looking around, but Hila was more cautious.

"What if the ramp should close while we were inside? We don't know how to open it from inside the ship." She suggested that they study the symbols on the outside, as best they could, then one of them would go inside and try to find the same symbols there. If they could they would try to open and close it with one person inside and one outside.

Arina saw the wisdom in this and suggested that she go inside and look around. Hila would remain outside and open the ramp from there if necessary.

Arina made her way cautiously up the ramp and into the ship. Although the Elders were no more than five feet tall and quite slim, the interior was obviously designed for creatures somewhat smaller. Arina did her best to maneuver around at the top of the ramp without touching anything. She tried to imagine what the area would look like when the ramp was closed. Then she looked for some symbols like those on the exterior of the ship. There was nothing visible in the eerie dim red light.

"I'm going to look around for some other symbols," she called down to Hila. "If the ramp closes, just go ahead and open it"

Arina was in the lower level of the ship. There was a pole that led through an opening in the ceiling to an upper level. Arina took hold of it and pulled herself up. The surface was rough, which aided her grip. The next level was larger and there appeared to be several rooms leading off of the central passageway. Some doors were open, others closed. As she was pulling herself up, Arina saw many symbols scattered around the walls and by the doors. But when she was finally standing on the center deck, all of the symbols had vanished.

Arina shook her head in disbelief. She knew she had seen the symbols. What had happened to them? She went over to a door and looked carefully around for some hint of the symbols. Nothing. As she was looking around, she bumped her head on a pipe that was traversing the ceiling. Besides causing pain, the incident sparked a sudden realization. Whoever this ship belonged to weren't as tall as the Elders. Maybe if she were shorter...

She squatted down and looked back at the doorway. There were the symbols, plain as day.

She stood up and looked again where she knew they were – she could not see them. Lesson one: the labels were designed to be seen from only one perspective. Above or below that point they were invisible to the Elder's eyes. Arina made a mental note that when they came back they should bring stools to sit on.

Arina went to the pole and dropped down to the lower level again. Then she squatted down and started looking again for the ramp instructions. It took a while, but she finally found them on the far side of what may have been an airlock. She took a deep breath and pressed on what she thought was the 'close' symbol.

The airlock door slid silently closed and the ramp retracted back into the bottom of the ship. Arina waited, quite nervously, for Hila to extend the ramp. But the ramp remained retracted and the airlock door closed. Arina became even more nervous. What if Hila had gone back to the Valley, or had somehow been injured when she had closed the ramp? She tried pressing on the 'open' symbol, but nothing happened. There was a clear panel in the airlock door. Arina could see the closed ramp. Why wouldn't the door open? She looked around for some sort a symbol that looked promising, but could see nothing that she really wanted to try.

Panic was about to break out when there was a subtle hiss and Arina could see the ramp extending through the airlock door. But the airlock remained firmly closed. Okay, it was now time to panic. Arina noted that she was breathing much more rapidly than usual. She tried to consciously slow her breathing, to relax. Relaxation came, but her breathing didn't slow. If she squinted just right, she could see Hila at the bottom of the ramp. She was trying to say something, but the sound didn't make it through the airlock.

There had to be another switch! Arina searched the area near the airlock. Then she saw it – a bit off to the side. She couldn't quite make out the symbol, but it had to be the right one. There was nothing else in the vicinity that it could control. Arina pressed it with crossed fingers. At first, nothing happened. Then the airlock silently slid open and Arina dropped through and stumbled down the ramp taking in deep breaths of fresh air.

Hila waited until Arina's breathing had normalized and then she peppered her with questions. Arina had only one question – why had Hila taken so long to extend the ramp?

"I'm sorry," Hila explained. "But I just had to empty my bladder and was off looking for a proper place to do it. As soon as I returned and saw the ramp retracted I opened it back up. But I only have the one switch. It must be designed so that the little door can only be opened or closed from the inside."

Lesson two: the ramp can be extended from the outside, but the airlock can only be opened or closed from inside the ship. (Safety feature?) To extend the ramp from inside the ship, first open the airlock.

Lesson three: Leave ramp extended and airlock open while working inside the ship. A fan to circulate the air would be a good idea, if there were electricity to run it.

They made a note to ask Enela about the fan idea, maybe there would be something in the supply bunker that would do the job. In the meantime the two sat down and planned their approach to unraveling the mysteries of the ship. Before they did anything else they would have to map out the interior of the ship and the location and design of all the symbols they could find. Perhaps they would be able to see a pattern. Even the thought of the magnitude of the project was enough to boggle their minds.

The next morning Hila and Arina stopped by the supply bunker, but Enela was not there. The new attendant, Niana, did not know where Enela was, only that she had been summoned to take over the job. Hila and Arina spent some time poking around among the various supplies. In the end they had managed to find two small fans, some electric cord and even some photoelectric cells. There was no way to know if the cells would provide enough power for the fans, but it was the best they could devise. They also opted for a digital camera.

On the way back to the cave, they stopped by the Council chamber, only to find it empty. So they proceeded on, still wondering at Enela's fate.

Once back at the cave they placed the photoelectric cells at the edge of the opening they had made in the rock face and set up the fans in the ship. As long as the arrays were in direct sunlight they generated just enough power to spin the two fans. They didn't spin rapidly, but they did turn enough to keep the air moving. Hila and Arina hoped that would be sufficient.

As soon as the fans were working, the two set about their task. Making a careful and detailed note of the location and character of each symbol they could find. Hila tried adding digital photos to their notes, but she had a problem working out the proper flash settings. Too often the flash would wash out the symbol. Eventually she discovered that a distant shot would mute the flash and the zoom would capture the symbol. She soon had a camera full of images.

Besides the entrance, they discovered that the lower level of the ship contained a large storage room. Though the room seemed to be completely empty, the smell in that room was horrible. They exited almost immediately.

There being nothing more of interest on the lower level, the two made their way up to the mid level. Here the pole led to a round central corridor opening onto several rooms. They picked one at random and opened the door. It looked like a combination dining and cooking facility. There was a table surrounded by several seats, counter space on which appeared to be some sort of oven. There were even flat pieces of metal, which could have served as dishes and some devices that could have served as utensils.

They went on to the next room and found several cots suspended from the walls. There were some interesting artifacts scattered about the room. They could not even imagine the use to which they might be put. Hila picked up a small cube and a sound suddenly emanated from it. It startled Hila and she dropped the object onto the floor. The sound stopped. Out of curiosity Arina picked it up and the sound began again. It certainly didn't sound like any music she had ever heard, but it might be a spoken language. There were no marks on the cube to give a hint as to its purpose. They put it back on the floor and headed to the next room.

That room was even small than the other two. The rear of the room looked like the inside of a toaster, with wires arranged in horizontal rows along both walls. In the front of the room was a strange apparatus set off to one side. It was raised up from the floor, a bit longer than wide and had a hole in the top of it. They looked at it, trying to figure out what it might be used for. Then Arina got an idea. She walked over to the device and straddled it.

"A toilet?" exclaimed Hila. "Well, why not. I suppose they would have to have one. How does it work?"

"I don't know," answered Arina. She stood to one side and peered into the opening. "I see some of those wires inside," she said, indicating the wires at the back of the room. "Do you suppose they had a way of disintegrating the waste?"

Hila thought for a moment. "If the wires are used to disintegrate things, what do you suppose those over there are used for?"

"Well, if they worked at a lower strength," Arina surmised, "maybe they are the equivalent of a shower. You know, burning off any microbes or dirt without harming the skin."

Neither of them really liked the idea of being toasted clean.

Hila made a record of all the symbols and switches around the room. She even tried one or two, but nothing seemed to be working. Eventually they gave up and moved on the last door.

As soon as the door opened, the two gasped. "Jackpot!" exclaimed Hila. There in front of them was what could only be described as the control room. There was a large console situated against the outside wall with two chairs by it. There were two other consoles along the side walls. Each had its own chair. In the center of the room was a single chair on a raised dais. The whole thing looked like an imitation of the bridge of the Enterprise.

There were many gauges and screens, levers and touch pads and dials. There were symbols all over the place. Somewhere in here had to be the switch that would turn on the power for the entire ship. But where?

The two just stood at the door, stunned by the complexity of the job ahead. Finally, Hila said, "Okay, we've seen this room. Lets see what's in the penthouse."

They went back into the central corridor and looked for a way up. There was none. The pole stopped at the ceiling. This was another puzzle. They went back through each of the rooms looking for some exit to the upper level and found nothing. They even examined a few cabinets and storage compartments in the control room. But there was no way up.

"What about this?" Arina asked, pointing to small door in the wall of the central area. It looked like some sort of storage cabinet. Hila shrugged and went over to open it. When she looked about the door she could see a number of symbols. They sort of looked like warning signs, although she couldn't make out what they indicated. Another shrug and she pressed the latch.

The door opened onto what appeared to be a small machine room. It was full of cables and pipes. On the far wall was a ladder. There wasn't any ceiling. The room opened up into the upper level. Getting into the room was another chore. Hila could just barely squeeze through the door. Once inside there was barely enough room to turn around and make her way to the ladder. She climbed up for a look around.

The upper level was filled with machinery of some kind. There were large and small cabinets and boxes and barrels. All linked by cables and pipes. This was obviously the engine room. There were no controls or gauges in evidence here, so she climbed down and attempted to squeeze back out the door to the corridor.

As Hila was describing what she had seen, Arina suddenly stopped her, holding a finger to her lips. The two listened. There was nothing but silence. Silence! They should have been able to hear the fans. They leaped for the pole and slid down to the lower level. Then fans were not running. Hila and Arina sprinted down the ramp, not wanting to repeat Arina's earlier experience with the fetid air in the ship.

Once they were outside the ship, the cause of the fan's stopping was obvious. It was ominously dark outside. Clouds were rolling in and it looked like an afternoon of storms was in the offing.

"Looks like we're out of business for the rest of the day," said Hila. "Let's close up shop and go back to the Valley. I'm sure that the Councilors will want to see these pictures." With that they removed the fans, closed the entrance ramp and made their way back to the Valley.

Hila and Arina stopped at the Council chamber, but again it was empty. There was nothing to do but wait until a Councilor stopped by, so they settled in for a long wait. When no one had shown up by evening, they took turns going out to the toilet and to get some food and water. After a few more hours they gave up and went to get some sleep.

The next morning the Council chamber was buzzing. All five Councilors were there. Enela was sitting over to one side with the instruction manual in her hands. Billy Eagle, the reservation sheriff was standing with the Councilors talking to them quite animatedly. There was also another human in the group whom Hila and Arina didn't recognize immediately. After a few minutes, Hila gasped, "That's Red Hawk!" And so it was, but she was dressed in simple human clothing and not her traditional buckskins.

Hila and Arina moved quietly over to Enela and sat down beside her.

"What's up?" Hila whispered.

"Apparently there was a big to-do in Winton yesterday" Enela answered. "From what I've been able to gather, Ari-Ana and Ari-Nia asked Billy to take them to Winton yesterday to do some shopping. While they were there they bumped into Professor Gauss at one of the stores. I'm not sure just what happened, but apparently he made a big stink and suggested that they go back to the desert and not bother 'normal' people.

"You know that Ari-Ana wouldn't take that too kindly. Anyway when things escalated, Billy stepped in to come to the Councilors' rescue. That really ticked Gauss off and he called Billy an

93

'injun' and told him to stay on the reservation where he belonged. Someone finally called the local police and Dr. Archer had to intercede to keep Ari-Ana and Ari-Nia from being booked into the jail. It was a real mess!"

"Wow!" Hila said. "If they had discovered that Ari-Ana and Ari-Nia weren't human, we would all have been in deep doo-doo. What's going to happen, now?"

"Billy and Red Hawk seem to think that Ari-Ana and Ari-Nia should just ignore the whole affair and ditch the disguises they were wearing. They gave the police phony names and addresses, so they can't be traced. Even if the judge issues a warrant for their arrest, the police will never be able to find them.

"But Ari-Ana wants to go back and erase some memories. Red Hawk and Billy are trying to convince her that is a very bad idea. If they should be caught again, they wouldn't be able to get them off without jail time."

"So what do *we* do?" Arina just wasn't interested in human problems when she had a strange spacecraft to investigate.

"Ari-Ana brought back a generator and some larger fans," Enela said. "We can lug all the stuff over to the cave and continue exploring the space ship."

The other two picked up on the idea until they saw the amount of 'stuff' Ari-Ana had purchased. It was all the three of them could do to carry it out of the Valley and into the cave. They set the generator up near the opening in the rock wall and stretched the extension cords to allow them to put fans in to lower level of the ship and in the control room door. Once it was all hooked up and the generator was humming quietly, they retired to the control room.

"Ari-Ula and I finished the translation of the first page yesterday," Enela explained. "It said that the ship had been damaged in some sort of a battle and could not be flown. There were no details, but there were explicit orders not to try to fly the ship or to retract the legs. It seems to have a gyroscope problem."

"So, if we cant fly it, what good is it?" Arina asked.

"I still have several pages of instructions to translate." Enela said. "Whoever wrote the text kept the language pretty simple and included a lot of diagrams. It should get easier as I go along."

"Does it say how to turn on the power?" Hila always looked on the practical side.

"Actually, I think it does," said Enela. "Look here at page three."

Enela scanned the page and recognized the word 'power' and some simple instructions. Also on the page was a drawing of the appropriate console and the location of the necessary switches. But there was no scale to the drawing, nor was there any indication as to where the console was, not how much of the console was contained in the drawing. Whoever made the drawing did not bother to include any of the alien symbols.

Looking about the control room, it was obvious that finding the correct switch was not going to be easy. Enela, Hila and Arina began examining each of the consoles looking for a switch configuration that might match the one on the page. Very soon, the scope of the problem became painfully obvious. Each of them had found two or three configurations each of which was similar to that on the page. The three worked diligently to rule out as many of the possibilities as they could, but they thought that there were still too many to risk trying any.

It was Arina who had the first inspiration. "So far," she said at last, "the only thing on this ship that seems to have any power connection is the entry ramp and the lighting. Though I have yet to see any source for this hideous red light. None of the controls appear to have any power going to them – at least all of the displays and gauges are dark."

"And your point is … ?" asked Hila, who was quickly getting frustrated by their lack of progress.

"Why can't we just try the best possibilities?" Arina continued, ignoring Hila for the moment. "If the control room has no power, then the only switch that should be able to do anything is the power switch."

Hila and Enela just looked at one another and then back to Arina. It was so simple! They reviewed the possible power switches that they had identified. One was on the 'Captain's chair' as they had dubbed the seat on the dais. They ruled that out – navigation, communication or weapons, maybe – but not a simple power switch. Another was on the main control panel, but that was in a prominent position, right in the middle of everything, not somewhere one would expect to find a one-time only switch.

They settled on a switch located on the right side panel. Arina poised her hand over the switch, but couldn't bring herself to actually press it. The other two watched intently, mentally willing her to press the switch. Finally, it was Enela who intervened. With an exasperated, "Oh, piff!" she reached over and activated the switch. Nothing happened.

Emboldened by Enela's act, Hila went to the left side console and promptly pressed the next candidate. Again there was no reaction from the ship. The three then proceeded to try each of the other possibilities, even the one on the Captain's chair. None of the switches turned on the power – neither did they do anything harmful. Back to square one.

"Okay," said Arina, "let's tackle this problem logically. If you were going to install a power switch, where would you put it?"

"By the power source?" offered Hila.

"No good," said Enela. "The power source is too hard to get to. That would be impractical. In the human houses, they put the switches by the door of the room."

Hila and Arina thought for a second. Then both jumped up simultaneously bolted out the door toward the center pole.

"Whoa!" shouted Enela. "It's not likely to be down by the ramp." The other two pulled up short and looked back at Enela. How dare she pour cold water on their great idea!

"The instructions said that the ship was involved in a battle of some sort," Enela pointed out. "If I were about to be boarded by a hostile force, I would not want them to have access to my power switch while I was still trying to fight them off."

Hila and Arina slowly made their way back into the control room. As they passed the threshold they turned and scanned the walls beside the door. They squinted and screwed up their noses, but all they could find was the switch to activate the door.

"It has to be easily accessible to the crew," Enela was musing, almost to herself, "hard for the enemy to get to and out of the way of normal operations. Think of the power switch on a computer … " She looked around the control room, trying to find a spot that would fit those requirements. Then, as if to verify an assumption, she asked, "Which side of the doors are the switches on?"

Arina thought for a second, but Hila looked back at the door of the control room. "On the left," she said. But Enela was already moving to the left side of the center console. She bent over and examined the side where it jutted out from the wall of the room. Then she reached down and pressed the side of the console.

There was no immediate response. Then a gentle hum could be heard as the electronic components began coming to life. There was no blinding flash of light. In fact the light remained at a low red glow. Obviously, the aliens had different eyes than the Elders. Enela, at least, found the dull red lighting hard on her eyes and difficult to see in.

Within a minute the gauges and dials were registering things and the large screen on the far wall was giving off a low glow. The three Elders just stood back and took it all in.

"Okay," said Arina. "We have power. What's next?"

"Well," Hila offered, "we sure don't want to go around and try pressing switches at random any more."

"I don't know," Enela said. "I'm going to have to translate more of the instructions. And I have another session with Red Hawk this afternoon. I may even be late now … You two are going to have to continue trying to decipher the symbols. I'll get back to you when I have something." With that Enela made her way out of the ship and back to the Valley. Even if she tried to act nonchalantly, there was something of a skip to her step. She was definitely feeling the results of an endorphin rush.

Enela was not late for her session with Red Hawk. In fact she was sufficiently early to have plenty of time to visit a toilet and get some food and water to fortify her for the afternoon's trials.

She wanted to ask Red Hawk about the events of the previous day, but Red Hawk was not in the mood to dwell on the past, except for Enela's past. She quickly and smoothly coerced Enela into a trance. The next thing Enela knew as she came out of the trance was that some two hours had gone by. That was more than twice the time they usually spent.

The only thing that Red Hawk would say when Enela pressed her for some hint as to her progress was that it was still too early to tell anything. But she left Enela with the tantalizing comment that she, Enela, was indeed a very remarkable person.

After her time with Red Hawk, Enela wandered back to the supply bunker. It was still early enough to try another call to Mary. She selected a different cell phone – no sense in using up the minutes and battery of one phone. Went out to her spot by the trees and dialed Mary's number.

This time Mary herself answered. Enela could hear Mary tell her father that it was Linda on the line. His response did not sound all that disagreeable. Mary told Enela that when she and her father had gone shopping the other day she had purchased her own cell phone. She gave Enela the new number. Now Enela could call without having to deal with the Professor. Enela asked about the melee in Winton the other day.

"When I heard about it I thought that it might have involved you or your family," Mary said. "But I wasn't there and father just ranted about how 'those people' were trying to take over everything; how they weren't staying out where they belonged; that they had no business coming into Winton with the white people. He was really in a foul mood." Then Mary hesitated for a moment. "You know I don't feel that way! Especially about you … "

Enela quickly changed the subject and they went on and on about nothing and everything for quite some time. When they finally broke off the conversation, Enela went back into the supply bunker where she could settle down with a lantern to translate page four of the manual.

The next day was overcast and rainy. It reflected Enela's mood. Despite the hours she had spent on the manual the previous night, she had made little progress. The one thing she had discovered was that the page contained what appeared to be the combination to a sealed locker on the ship. She turned the operation of the supply bunker over to Niana and made her way to the cave.

She found the rocks quite slippery and took her time climbing up to the opening. The rain had blown into the cave and Enela nearly took a header climbing down the debris inside. The ship was still sealed. Neither Hila nor Arina had made it yet. There wasn't enough light outside to operate the fans, so Enela dispensed with them and simply opened the ship and made her way up to the central level. There, to the left of the control room was the locker. They had tried the door earlier but found it completely secure. Now Enela had the key and she was going to find out what secret it concealed. She hoped that whatever was inside would help her translate the page.

Beside the door was a flat pad with some symbols on it. But those symbols were not on the page. It was infuriating! Whoever wrote the instructions insisted on using nothing but the Elder language and symbols. Why couldn't they have simply shown the alien characters and symbols? So far Enela and her companions had learned that the aliens had a 16-based number system and tended to write from right to left. She did a little figuring and translated the Elder symbols into what should have been the alien numbers. She took a deep breath and pressed the appropriate symbols on the keypad.

Nothing happened. The door was still locked. Enela looked for some sort of an unlocking switch. Nothing was obvious. The keypad had four rows of four symbols each. There were no special switches. Enela rechecked her translation. She was sure of her work. It had to be the arrangement of the symbols on the keypad. Did the aliens write numbers differently from letters? Nothing ventured – nothing gained. Enela started going over the various possibilities. On her third attempt there was a soft 'click' and the door opened. Note for posterity: the aliens arrange keypads vertically from left to right.

Just as the door opened Hila and Arina arrived.

"What's up?" Hila asked. "How did you get that open?"

"The combination was on the fourth page of the manual," Enela explained, showing her the sheet. "I hope that the contents will help me translate the page."

Arina opened the door fully. Inside there were several items that looked suspiciously like weapons. Enela let out a low whistle, then yelled, "Hila, don't!" as the latter was reaching into the locker.

"There are a lot of negatives on this page," Enela explained. "I have a feeling that these fall into the category of 'look – don't touch', at least until we get a better handle on how they work and what they do. I don't think Ari-Ana would be very happy if we blew a hole in this ship or killed someone. Take a picture so I can study it as I translate this page and let's close this up until we know what we're doing."

Arina was shocked. "You actually sound sensible for a change, Enela. Let's do just that." Then after a pause, she added, "And let's not tell anyone what we found. I think I would feel safer if these things are safely locked up in here where no one can get at them."

The other two looked at Arina with some concern, but neither pursued the subject. They took the pictures and resealed the locker. Then Enela explained to the other two how the alien's number system worked. Then she took the camera and retreated back to the supply bunker to study the manual. Arina and Hila went to review the control room gauges in light of the new information.

It took several hours and a lot of trial and error before Enela was satisfied with her translation. She knew how the weapons worked and the kind of damage they could inflict. They could emit a combination laser and sonic pulse. In space the pulse would continue until it ran into something. At that point it would act as a – the word that came to mind was one she had heard in a science fiction film – a disruptor. It would essentially destroy a portion of what it hit. More or less depending on its consistency. If it hit the torso of a person, there would be a head and pieces of the legs left over. If it hit solid granite, a single burst would probably cut out a melon-size hole. In the earth's atmosphere a pulse would eventually dissipate due to air friction. But that would take a long distance, maybe some 300 yards or more. There was supposed to be a non-lethal setting. Enela wondered who had volunteered to test that out.

The page indicated that there were five weapons on the ship, one for each crewmember. They were stored in the cabinet in charging blocks. A full charge was good for several hundred pulses. Enela looked at the pictures again. She could make out the trigger and another switch on the side of the weapon that probably altered the strength of the pulse. She was about to put the photos away, when something caught her eye. There were indeed five weapons placed in what looked like a charging block. But, there were two other weapons laid in the back of the locker, not in charging blocks. A total of seven weapons! Where had the other two come from? She rechecked the manual page. No, it was quite clear that there should be five weapons. Enela suddenly began to feel a little uncomfortable about the whole situation.

It was getting to be late in the afternoon. Enela decided against going back to the cave. Instead she sought out a toilet and then went to get some food and water. She returned to the supply bunker and placed a call to Mary's cell phone. There was no answer and Enela ended up talking to Mary's voice mail. Then she went back to translating the last section of the instruction manual. It took up several pages and obviously dealt with a particular part of the control room. There were many numbers and diagrams involved. Very shortly Enela's head was swimming in very deep water. Enela did not sleep well that night. She kept having dreams of exploding melons and molten rock.

Chapter 9

Worm Hole

The next day dawned bright and sunny. Enela's spirits should have rebounded accordingly, but she was still concerned over the previous day's discoveries and upset that she hadn't been able to talk with Mary. She spent some time reviewing her translations of the previous night while she was handing out supplies. It was late in the morning when she made her way over to the cave to locate the mysterious panel in the control room. As she approached the butte, she noticed something lying on the ground. She picked it up and found a neatly folded newspaper. Enela looked around to see who might have dropped it, but there was no one to be seen and no reason for a newspaper to be anywhere in the vicinity. She figured that Hila or Arina had dropped it on their way to the cave, so she tucked it under her arm and continued to the cave.

Hila and Arina were already working in the ship when Enela arrived. "Okay, who dropped the newspaper?" Enela asked.

"Hello to you, too," said Arina. "What newspaper?"

"This one," Enela said, holding up the folded paper.

"Not mine," said Hila.

"Ditto," Arina echoed.

"That's funny," Enela mused. "I found it laying on the ground next to the butte. Who could have put it there but one of us? Has there been anyone nosing around?"

"No one that I have heard of," said Hila. And again Arina concurred. "Is it today's paper?"

Enela unfolded the paper and looked at the date. She stood there staring at the paper for some time.

"Well?" asked Hila.

"What day is it today?" Enela asked.

"It's the 21st, Tuesday." Arina answered. "Why?"

"This paper says it was printed on Saturday, the 25th. This has to be some kind of a joke!"

"What!"

"Let me see that!"

The three spent the next several minutes looking the paper over for some sign of a joke or prank. But there was none that they could find. They quickly searched every page of the paper. The ads all touted weekend specials. The dates in the comic panels all read 9/21. None of them was really up on current events, so the news of the day made little impact; but none of it sounded so far off base as to be suspicious. Arina even commented that no one had claimed the lotto prize again that week.

Then, Enela stepped back, a strange expression on her face. She quietly gathered up the last few pages of instructions that she had dropped in her haste to look at the newspaper. She flipped through the pages, searching; then she looked up. "That must be it," she said quietly.

Hila and Arina looked at her, startled as much by the sudden quiet as by the expression on Enela's face.

"What's 'it'?" Arina asked. Then she looked at Hila, who also now bore a weird expression. "Are you two all right?"

"It's in the instructions," Enela almost whispered. "I misread them last night. They don't say 'speedy travel' . They say 'time travel'! *We* must have put that newspaper there some time *after* Saturday."

Arina was still holding the newspaper, but now she let it slowly fall from her fingers into a crumpled heap on the floor. They all just looked at it

Hila was the first to speak, "But how … ?"

"It's explained here in the last pages of the instructions … sort of," Enela was stilled overwhelmed as much by the latest finding as by her inability to see it last night.

"Are you sure this is a time machine? Arina asked. "It still looks just like a space craft of some sort." She was ever the pragmatist.

"It's the navigation system," Enela explained. "It generates wormholes. They are how the spaceship maneuvers through light years of space in a few moments. But the system in this spaceship has additional settings that can be used to move backward in time as well as forward through space. We know we can't fly it because of the gyroscope problem, but we can use the navigation system to generate a wormhole backward in time."

Hila and Arina weren't convinced. "Maybe we ought to show this to Ari-Ana," Hila suggested. No one disagreed, so the three set off for the Valley and the Council Chamber. They walked in silence, each mulling over the possibilities that the newspaper portended.

When they arrived, the Council Chamber appeared to be deserted. They looked around, found nobody home and were about to leave when Ari-Ana walked in.

"Well, what brings you here at this hour? Red Hawk isn't due for another hour or two, Enela. And I thought that you two were working on the strange ship…"

"I finished translating the manual, Ari-Ana, and we found something this morning that we felt you should see," Enela said, and she handed the newspaper to Ari-Ana.

Ari-Ana looked at the paper and saw nothing unusual, then she saw the date. "Is this some sort of a joke?"

"We thought so, too, at first," Arina said. "But we couldn't find anything wrong with it. It appears to be truly genuine."

"And I am sure that we have no newsprint in the supply bunker, nor a printing press." Enela added. "The closest one I know of is in Winton. I don't know of anyone in the Valley or on the reservation who could have made this up." Then she hastily continued, "And there were no signs of any humans on this side of the butte where I found the paper."

Ari-Ana considered what had been said as she continued to look over the paper. "Does your latest translation shed any light on this, Enela?"

"It may, Ari-Ana," Enela explained. "The last part of the manual discusses the use of a piece of navigation equipment … "

"I thought that the ship could not be flown," Ari-Ana interrupted. "Of what use is navigation equipment?"

"There is a phrase in the manual that mentions 'time travel' … " Enela offered tentatively, not knowing exactly how Ari-Ana would take it.

"Time travel?!" as Enela feared, Ari-Ana was incredulous.

"Well, we haven't had the chance to evaluate the instructions, yet. But if the newspaper is genuine, how else do you explain it?" Enela wasn't about to be turned off this time.

"Please evaluate those instructions at the earliest possible opportunity. In the meantime I will hang onto the newspaper. Oh, and, Enela, don't forget your session with Red Hawk this afternoon." With that, Ari-Ana turned and moved off to her private chamber.

"Okay, let's get going," said Arina. And she and Hila turned to head back to the butte.

"I can't go now," Enela complained. "I have that stupid session with Red Hawk. I'm going to take a leak and get some lunch. Why don't we get started first thing tomorrow morning?" Then she had some second thoughts and leafed through the instruction manual.

"Look, here is the panel for the navigation system. See if you can find it and work out any of the displays and controls. The instructions aren't too clear about the ordinary functions. There is supposed to be some sort of a stellar display connected with it. That should keep you busy this afternoon. But, whatever you do, don't try to generate any wormholes. You might accidentally end up in some strange galaxy where they breathe methane or something."

That last comment elicited a giggle from Hila, and a look of utter disdain from Arina. But they agreed not to do anything of consequence until they could get together with the manual in the morning. Hila and Arina went back to the butte and Enela headed off to find a toilet and some fungus to munch on.

Once she had emptied her bladder and filled her stomach, Enela lolled about for a while under a pine tree and pondered the mystery of the newspaper. She kept coming back to Arina's comment about the lottery. That no one had claimed the grand prize this week. Enela had scanned the lottery results summary where the paper had printed the winning numbers for the week. She intentionally recalled the article, making sure that she could picture the winning numbers. She had only a general knowledge of the lottery, but she knew that it was possible to win a lot of money if you picked the right numbers. Enela didn't really have any need for money – everything she needed was readily available in the Valley. And she did not fancy trying to live outside the Valley. Then again, with a lot of money …

Her reverie was suddenly shattered when she realized that it was time for her session with Red Hawk. She got up and sprinted off to the Council Chamber.

Red Hawk was waiting patiently in an empty conference room when Enela arrived. As usual, she was in a deep trance. Enela settled down on the floor opposite Red Hawk and waited for her to acknowledge Enela's presence.

"So," said Red Hawk after a few minutes, "I understand that you are making great progress in deciphering the Elder language."

"Yes," Enela admitted, "I have completed a first draft of the material. Most of it seems to be accurate, so far. I only have one section to wrap up. We'll start on that tomorrow. But, I do have a question … "

"Another problem with mythology?" Red Hawks voice was always calm, her speech well measured.

"No, this time it has to do with science – physics and astronomy, I guess," Enela was wondering how to phrase her question without sounding absolutely stupid. "It has to do with time travel …"

"Well, I'm not exactly a scientist," Red Hawk answered. "Just what is your question?"

Enela decided to just jump right in. "Well, if a person could travel forward in time and learn that something had not happened. Could that person then travel back in time and make it happen – even if it hadn't?"

Red Hawk sat in silence for two or three minutes, apparently contemplating the problem.

"As I said, I am no scientist, but I have read a bit about this very subject. Most physicists and astronomers agree that time travel is theoretically possible, if an appropriate wormhole can be established. But they also agree that it would be impossible to travel forward in time."

"But what if it *could* be done?" Enela persisted. "Could someone actually change the future?"

"That's a different question," Red Hawk answered. "There are several levels of paradoxes associated with time travel. For example, would it be possible for a person to travel back in time and kill his own grandfather while he was still a young boy? If he did, what would happen to him? Or what would happen if a person went back in time and accidentally killed himself? Or even shook his own hand? Modern theory is that there may well be several different time lines. These time lines may exist simultaneously and even connect to one another at different critical junctures. Are you thinking about the newspaper you found this morning?"

"Yes," Enela knew that there was no hope of concealing anything from Red Hawk. "There was an article that said that there was no winner in the weekly lottery game. The article gave the winning numbers. What if someone bought a ticket with those numbers?"

"You feel the need for a lot of money just now?" Red hawk asked with just the slightest trace of a smile.

"No, not me personally. I just thought that maybe with enough money we could get the spaceship working again … "

Red Hawk's attitude seemed to become more stern. "First, I don't know of anyone among the Elder people who has the knowledge to fix the ship, given any amount of money. Secondly, if any human ever found out about the ship they would seize it immediately, and the Elder people would be found out. I can't think of anything more disastrous. Now, shall we get on with our session?"

Red Hawk was finding it easier and easier to place Enela into a trance. She didn't even have time to answer Red Hawk's last question before her mind was floating in the middle of a void. In what seemed like the blink of an eye her mind was back in the present again and Red Hawk was thanking her for her cooperation.

"Are you really learning anything useful from all these sessions?" Enela asked.

"Oh, indeed I am!" Red Hawk assured Enela. "We are now almost all the way back to the arrival of your people on this planet. Just one or two more sessions and we will see if you can remember anything of that period. Oh, I have another meeting to attend on Thursday, so I will see you again one week from today. Will that be all right?"

Enela agreed, and then headed back to the supply bunker. She desperately wanted to talk to Mary. It had been days since their last conversation.

When she got back to the bunker, Enela picked out a phone with plenty of power and minutes and settled down into a back corner. She dialed Mary's number and listened anxiously as the other phone rang … and rang … and … "

"Hello?" It was Mary's voice on the other end. Enela was ecstatic.

"Hi, it's Enela."

"Oh, hi. I was hoping you would call. Wait a minute." There were soft sounds on the other end and Enela could hear a door closing. "Okay, I'm back. I didn't want Daddy eavesdropping. What's up?"

"Not much. I'm still working on that special project. We may be about to complete it. Or at least move it into a different phase. What about you?"

"I just celebrated my seventeenth birthday. Daddy threw a big party. It lasted all evening. I do wish you could have been here."

"Oh, I did try to call, but there was no answer. That must have been the night of the party. Well, happy birthday! How does it feel to be seventeen?"

"To tell you the truth, I haven't noticed any real difference. Daddy is still a big pain. I wanted to invite some friends from school to the party, but they were the wrong color or the wrong economic class or the wrong something! Sometimes I just can't figure him out."

"Well, I have a birthday present for you." Enela had made up her mind. "Do you have a pencil and paper?" Another quick pause on the other end, then …"

"OK, shoot."

Enela pulled up the image of those winning lottery numbers and read them off to Mary. "Don't ask any questions, and don't ever tell anyone where you got those numbers. Just go buy

114

a ticket before Friday night. And let me know what happens."

The rest of the conversation was simply more 'girl talk', but Enela enjoyed every minute of it. When they finally said good night, Enela knew she was going to sleep very well, very well indeed.

Bright and early the next morning Enela, Arina and Hila met in the control room of the space ship. Arina and Hila had located the navigation panel the previous day and had even managed to display a star map. Now they proudly displayed their accomplishment to Enela. She looked at the display curiously, screwing up her nose as she tried to make some sense of it.

"If this was the last display, shouldn't we be in here somewhere?" Enela asked.

"I'm sure we are," Arina answered. "But I for one have never seen our sun mapped from a point well outside the solar system. This looks like a snippet of our portion of space. Think about it. If our galaxy was the equivalent of the Northern Hemisphere, and our arm of that galaxy the equivalent of the western United States, then this display would be something like Arizona. Do you think you could recognize this butte from a satellite image of all of Arizona? Especially if you didn't know which end was up!"

"Umm," Enela saw the logic of that statement. "Maybe the coordinate displays will give us a clue as to which blip is our sun." She pulled out the instruction manual and set about trying to translate the alien's displays into some sort of understandable coordinates.

In the meantime Arina and Hila worked with the display, trying to move it around or enlarge a portion of it. At one point, after trying a new option, Hila gave out a shriek. The other two looked in shock at a very blank display screen.

"What happened?" Arina asked with just a tinge of panic in her voice.

"I don't know," answered Hila. "I was just tweaking this control and everything went away."

"Well, tweak it back," Enela suggested. The other two turned and looked at her with such utter disgust that she quickly realized how unhelpful that suggestion had been. But, ultimately, that is just what they did. Nothing they did would relight the display. At last they agreed to shut the whole system down and bring it back up. The display still remained stubbornly blank.

Enela went back to the manual for some help. There were many instructions for inserting coordinates to manually set the system, but no hint as to how one would use the automated applications. But, since the ship could not actually be flown, that was not to be unexpected. She looked at the panel. There were several switches that were not illustrated in the manual. Hila and Arina were still studying the display panel. Enela called their attention back to the navigation panel.

"Did you figure out what any of these switches do?" she asked.

Hila turned back from the display panel where she had been sitting. In doing so, she also moved her arm from the edge of the navigation panel where she had been resting it. There, under her arm was another set of switches, set in the smooth surface of the panel. All six eyes focused on the exposed switches.

Enela was the closest to the switches. One in particular attracted her attention. "If everything blows up, blame me," she said and pressed a switch near the spot where Hila's elbow had been resting. The display sprang back into life still showing the same star map. The three young Elders breathed a collective sigh of relief. And each made a personal resolution to be more careful about where they leaned in the future.

Hila went back to studying the star map display while Enela and Arina started in on the coordinate displays. Even with the help of the instruction manual, the coordinate displays were difficult to understand. First, they all consisted of the alien characters. These had to be translated into something more familiar. And, to make things even more interesting, the aliens used a base 16 system. Fortunately, Enela had found a calculator that did hex-decimal computations in the supply bunker. This helped greatly.

Then there was the problem of what each number represented. Here, the instruction manual helped a bit by indicating what some of the numbers referred to. By the end of the day they had managed to translate and identify the upper bank of displays.

The next day things went much better. Hila had determined that the star map was really a galaxy map. She had been able to locate both Virgo and the Milky Way. With that information and the coordinate data, they were able to shift the galaxy map slightly by varying the numbers. Then Enela got more venturesome. She centered the Milky Way galaxy in the display and tried to zoom in on one of the arms. After a couple of failed attempts, she was actually successful. None of them was sufficiently familiar with star charts to locate the Earth's solar system. But they could marvel at the various displays that they brought up.

Then Arina had an idea. She had located a switch, which appeared to point to a log of prior entries. She activated the switch and pressed an associated 'left arrow'. The display didn't change. It was Hila who reminded the others that the aliens wrote from right to left. She suggested that they use the 'right arrow' to move backwards. This time the coordinate displays changed, as did the star chart. They stepped back through all the changes Enela had made. Then they looked at the location at which the ship had been before arriving at Earth.

The star map didn't change all that much for several different sets of coordinates. Apparently the ship had made several stops in the area of the solar system. Then an entirely different map appeared in the display. The three just stared at the display. There was no way they could know what they were looking at. But it was obvious that this map bore no relation to the previous one. It was then that the realization really sunk in that they were in a ship that had traveled millions of miles through space.

Of course the Elders themselves were proof that there were different intelligent humanoid races living in the universe, but they had been so isolated on the Earth that this concept seemed strange to them. Now it came to the fore and it was very humbling.

Staring at the various star charts was interesting, but not very helpful. The three had a much more urgent task at hand and time was the one thing they could not waste. In a few days they had to transmit a copy of the Winton newspaper back in time so that Enela could find it as she had done on Wednesday.

At this point it seemed that they had enough information to actually establish a wormhole. They checked their findings and the operation of the various dials, gauges, switches and displays. No matter how sure they were, they checked everything all over again. Finally, they could delay no longer. It was time to run a real test. But how? They all agreed they could not just aim for a point out in space somewhere. Even if visiting another planet was an intriguing concept, they were hardly prepared for such a venture. It was Arina who suggested the first test.

"Let's set up a wormhole out in the open space between this butte and the Valley. Can we specify something about a hundred yards long? Then maybe we can just throw something through it … "

Hila and Enela immediately agreed and set about making the necessary measurements. They guesstimated that the center of the ship was about 25 meters inside the butte and that there was about another 5 meters of slag outside the opening. Enela made the necessary computations and conversions and started setting up the necessary displays. She set a length of 100 meters and situated the far end well away from any structure. It took almost half an hour to get everything just right and to double-check all the settings.

"How long do we want to leave the hole open?" Enela asked. "We don't want to leave it open too long, but we will need time to get outside and test it."

They decided that 15 minutes would be long enough to get outside and to throw something through the wormhole. A few more minutes of computing and converting and the last dial was set.

"Okay, everyone ready?" Enela asked. "Let's all push the switch together." The three gingerly positioned their hands above the switch. "On the count of three: one … two … "

"Wait!" Arina interrupted the countdown. "How do we know that we can generate a wormhole in an atmosphere or on the planet's surface? Everything we've seen indicates they were always generated in space."

Three hands instantly moved away from the switch. Hila, Enela and Arina just looked at one another. Arina was right. How did they know it was safe to generate a wormhole on the surface of a planet. Maybe it would suck off all the air, or cause some sort of a huge explosion. It was Hila who brought the group back into focus.

"Both ends of the wormhole are on the planet's surface, so it may cause some sort of a tornado or wind storm, but it's not going to suck off the atmosphere. Now as to an explosion, what does you instruction manual say about wormholes, Enela?"

Enela made a grab for the discarded manual pages and started madly flipping through them. At last she threw up her arms in despair.

"Nothing, apparently," she said. "No, wait …
" She was examining one particular page,
struggling to translate something. "There is a
caution here about setting the basic elevation too
low. I think it refers to getting the wormhole too
close to the ground. The example has a very small
number in it." She quickly scanned the settings on
the console and compared them to the manual
page. "Our basic elevation is greater than that in
the manual, so I think we are okay."

There was a collective sigh of relief and
again they positioned their hands over the switch.
This time, on 'three' , they each pressed the
switch.

There was no explosion. In fact there was no
sound at all. No bright lights. Nothing. For a
moment the three just looked at each other – then
they made a mad dash for the door of the control
room and ran outside the ship and to the opening
in the side of the butte.

They stood there, frozen to the spot, gazing
out into the desert toward the Valley. There,
suspended a foot or so above the ground some 10
meters from the butte was what appeared to be a
large ring of light shimmering in the afternoon
sun.

It took a minute or so for the realization to
sink in that they had just created a real, live
wormhole. Or at least the start of one. They
looked out toward the river where the tail end
should be, but saw nothing. The only anomaly in
the quiet dessert afternoon was the shimmering
ring.

"Come on, let's go!" cried Enela. "We don't
have a lot of time to test this thing."

They scrambled down the rocks to the floor of the dessert and made their way towards the wormhole. On the way, Enela picked up three large rocks and handed one to each of the others.

"Don't get too close," urged Arina. "We still don't know how these things work."

Hila carefully wandered beyond the visible opening so that she could look back at it from behind. As she passed the ring, it seemed to collapse down into a thin line. From the rear it was not visible at all. There was no indication that anything was even there. She could see Enela and Arina quite clearly. They appeared to be staring at something in front of them which simply wasn't there. She pointed this out to them and they switched places so that they could all appreciate the view from either side.

"That must be why we can't see the end of the wormhole," Enela mused. "We're looking at it from the wrong side. Well, let's test this thing."

They went back to the entry side of the wormhole.

"Enela, you go first," Arina still wasn't too sure about this whole process.

Enela moved about 2 meters away from the opening of the wormhole, hefted her rock a bit, then reared back and hurled it straight into the wormhole. There was a small spark when it hit the event horizon. Then the rock simply disappeared. Hila, who was standing at the edge of the hole saw Enela throw the rock and saw the rock enter the event horizon, but it never came out the other side.

Then the other two took their turns at throwing their rocks. The result was the same.

The rocks seemed to penetrate the horizon and the just disappeared. They just stared at the shimmering ring. Suddenly there was a bright flash followed by a very loud bang and a tremendous rush of air. All three jumped in panic as they were blown backward off their feet. It felt like a lightening bolt had just struck in front of them. But the sky was cloudless. They lay there for a moment, too numb to move.

Hila was the first to recover. "Wow! Now we know what it's like to create a wormhole in the atmosphere! That was awesome!"

"When it's created it must just displace the air." Arina pointed out. "Then, when it collapses, the displaced air rushes back in to fill the void."

"Let's go see if we can find our rocks," Enela suggested and set off toward the riverbed where she had supposedly placed the exit from the wormhole.

They searched for some time near the spot where the wormhole should have exited. The only remarkable thing they found was one badly beaten up cactus plant. They could only guess as to the cause of its condition. Perhaps, they surmised, it was too close to the wormhole. Still, they found no sign of the rocks.

Arina and Enela were quite dejected when there was no sign of the rocks. Arina, because she had been quite certain that the whole wormhole fiasco would never work. Now, although she felt quite satisfied that her original belief had been proven correct, there was no explanation for the appearance of the newspaper. Enela could not figure out what had gone wrong and was fretting that she had made some ghastly mistake.

Hila left the other two to their private musings. She started wandering in ever greater half-circles about the spot where the wormhole seemed to have ended. By the time the others noticed what she was doing she was already a good six meters from the wormhole exit. Suddenly she gave out with a shout.

"Here they are!"

Enela and Arina rushed out into the riverbed where Hila was standing. "We've got pretty good arms," she said as she pointed out the three rocks lying within a few feet of each other. "Apparently the wormhole doesn't reduce an object's inertia by very much."

They picked up the rocks. They were still warm from the afternoon sun. They also appeared to be in the same condition as when tossed into the wormhole.

By this time the sun was definitely on its way to the horizon. Hila, Enela and Arina wandered on back to the butte to secure the spaceship. As they walked in silence each was gently hefting a rock that had passed through a wormhole. When they returned to the Valley they went to the Council Chamber to meet with Ari-Ana and present her with three rather special new paperweights.

After emptying her bladder and harvesting some fungus for supper, Enela went back to the supply bunker. She was greatly enjoying her nightly phone calls to Mary. In fact, she was almost hooked on them. If she didn't get through to Mary, Enela was usually in a foul mood the next day. Tonight she was successful. Enela wanted very much to tell Mary all about her wormhole experiment. She had to bite her tongue when she absentmindedly mentioned the spaceship. She backpedaled furiously and pretended she was just talking about a dream.

Mary, on the other hand was still gloating about having her drivers license. Suddenly she suggested that she drive out to the dig site so she and Enela could meet in person again.

"You have your own car?" Enela asked, glad to change the subject, and even gladder at the possibility of meeting Mary again.

"No, father refuses to buy me one," Mary grouched. "But I can drive his. He's leaving on a two-day business trip Sunday afternoon. Suppose I drive him to the airport, then I can have the car. He'll never notice a few extra miles on it."

"Can you come out Sunday afternoon after you drop your father off?" Enela was pretty sure that Red Hawk would be taking the weekend off, and the newspaper problem would be resolved one way or another by then.

"Sure," Mary answered. "About 4:00 PM?"

"Great! I'll see you then," Enela's heart was soaring at the possibility. "Oh, by the way, did you buy that lottery ticket?"

"Yes, I did," Mary answered. "Maybe I'll even win a million dollars for us … "

Enela slept very well that night. She was quite confident that they could work out the rest of the problems and be ready to send the newspaper back to Wednesday by Saturday afternoon.

The next day the three started out early for the cave. As they were walking across desert separating the cave from the Valley they were

125

deep in conversation about the plans for the days work. The day would be spent working on the time travel problem. Setting up a wormhole was getting much easier, but adjusting the timing, especially for very short durations, was going to be quite tricky.

Suddenly, Arina cried out and the other two stopped in their tracks and turned toward her. She was holding her hand to her head and looking around.

"What happened?" asked Hila. Then she also yelled as a rock flew out of nowhere and missed her by inches. Enela looked around to see who might be throwing the rocks, but there was no one in sight. Then a third rock landed on the ground at her feet. Now they were all searching the surrounding desert, trying to find the source of the missiles. There was no one to be seen.

"I think they came from over by the cave," Enela said, searching the area carefully for some sign of activity. "Let's go see … "

They each grabbed a rock and headed toward the cave. They approached cautiously, still on the look out for more flying rocks. But there were none. And there was no sign that anyone else had been in the area. After a brief search, they gave up, pitched the rocks at the base of the pile and went on inside.

After some experimentation Enela finally thought that she had properly set up a wormhole to transport something back a ways in time. The three ran outside the cave to find the wormhole shimmering in the sunlight.

"Rocks again?" Arina asked, staring at the shimmering circle.

"Why not?" said Enela. "Here, we can use the same ones we found this morning." She picked up the three rocks and tossed one to each of the others.

"Okay, here goes," Arina reared back and let fly. The rock sailed through the wormhole and disappeared.

"Good toss!" Enela said. Then she had a second thought. "But maybe we shouldn't throw quite so hard this time … "

She and Hila threw their rocks into the wormhole with a bit less gusto. Just as Hila tossed her rock the wormhole gave a slight pop and disappeared.

"Okay," said Arina, "where was the exit of the wormhole this time? We had better go retrieve those rocks." She started off into the desert.

"I don't think you'll find them," said Enela. If everything worked as it was supposed to, we already found them."

"What?" Hila was a little slow catching on, but the expression on Arina's face clearly indicated that she had it figured out.

"Those were the rocks that came at us this morning, weren't they?"

"I think so," Enela admitted. "I tried to set the end of the wormhole about two hours ago. But I'm still not sure about the number translation. I may have missed it by several minutes."

"Let me get this straight," said Hila. The rocks we just threw were the ones that seemed to come at us this morning – out of nowhere? I didn't see any hint of the wormhole."

"Remember the one we set up yesterday?" Arina reminded the others. "None of us could see the entry point when we were standing behind it. Maybe you can't see the output end of a wormhole, either"

"So where are the rocks, now?" Hila always wanted a complete explanation.

"I don't know," Enela answered. "I suppose by now they are in our hands and we are bringing them back to the cave."

"But we're here. We can't be out there lugging the rocks back here at the same time."

"In our present we are here," Enela tried again. "But the rocks aren't here now, they are in our early morning. In our time they have already landed, been brought back here and we just tossed them back into the past. In our past they have landed and we are bringing them back here."

"But how can we be here and in the past at the same time?" Hila still wasn't convinced.

"We aren't," Enela tried to explain. "Think of time as kind of like a river. Normally we are just floating around in it flowing downstream. Suppose we found a piece of wood floating in the river and tossed it back upstream. Now it would be floating down the river behind us.

"Suppose we got out of the river, waited for a while and then got back in the river again. Our original time, and everyone who was floating along with us, would be far head of us downstream. Or suppose we walked back upstream before we got back in the river. Then we would not only lose the people who were originally floating with us, we would pass by the same sites that we had first seen all over again, but in new company. We can't move forward faster than the river is flowing. Even if we jumped out and tried to run along the bank, when we jumped back in we would just be where we started."

"That's fine," Arina said, "but how can we be in two places at the same time? Moreover, how could we be in the future lobbing rocks at ourselves and then lob rocks at ourselves in the past? How many of us are there?"

"There are just three of us," Enela answered with a slight grin. "But there could be a thousand time lines with the three of us in each one of them. Red Hawk told me that some scientists believe that a new time line breaks off whenever some significant event takes place. At each break a new time line is created. The old time line continues as though nothing had happened; but the event is crucial to the new time line.

"This morning we were on our way to the cave. When the first rock flew out of the wormhole and struck Arina, a new time line containing that incident was created and we were in it. When we threw the rocks into the wormhole we validated that event."

"But where are the rocks, now?" Hila was not going to be satisfied without wrapping everything up nice and neat.

"They are in a new timeline which we created by throwing them into the wormhole. Maybe in that timeline we don't come along just at the right time, maybe Arina isn't hit and we don't even notice the rocks. Every timeline is just a bit different from all the others similar to it."

"So what do we do now?" Arina asked.

"We practice setting up wormholes, so we can send back that newspaper tomorrow," Enela answered.

Chapter 10

It's Saturday

Saturday morning Enela, Arina and Hila went to the Council Chamber to meet with Ari-Ana. Somehow, today they would have to prove that the newspaper that Enela had stumbled upon Wednesday morning had indeed been sent to that spot from the future. Enela was sure that she understood the wormhole technology well enough to send the newspaper back in time. How to prove that the paper she sent back today was the same one she had found three days ago – that was another matter. Ari-Ana was waiting for them.

"Good morning!" Ari-Ana was in good spirits. "Are you ready for the big test?"

"Yes, Ari-Ana," Enela answered for all three. They had talked this over earlier and neither Arina nor Hila was sure that it was going to work.

"Then let's be off," Ari-Ana was carrying a folded newspaper.

They made their way out of the Valley and across the desert to the cave where the spaceship waited. No one spoke as they walked. Each person was keeping her own counsel. Once they were all crowded into the control room, Enela explained the process.

"I have set the wormhole to open outside the cave. We still don't trust trying to open a wormhole in the cave or in the spaceship. There is too much chance of something going very badly wrong. It will extend to a point about midway between the pueblo butte and the Valley, where I found the newspaper, and to a time early on last Wednesday morning. Is this agreeable to everyone?"

"It sounds fine, Enela," said Ari-Ana. "show me how you establish such a wormhole."

Enela was ready for this. She had already worked out all of the settings and wasted no time in entering them into the navigation system. Ari-Ana watched with great interest as Enela selected the various fields and entered the strange numbers. Finally, she was ready.

"Everything is set," Enela said with some resignation. "I will set the wormhole to last for 15 minutes. That will give us time to get outside and toss the newspaper through. May I have the paper?"

Ari-Ana handed the paper to Enela. As soon as her fingers touched the paper, Enela sensed that something was very wrong. She didn't even have to look at the date on the paper.

"This isn't the newspaper I found in the desert!" she exclaimed. "It's far too new!"

"That's right," Ari-Ana affirmed. "I asked Gray Wolf to bring me a copy from Wakulla as soon as they were delivered. I did not want anything to happen to the one you brought me. If you threw that into the wormhole, it would be gone forever."

"But, if this isn't the same paper, how can we be sure that what I gave you actually came from the future?"

"We can't, can we," Ari-Ana had her own agenda, and it certainly wasn't to corroborate the story that Enela had told. "Now shall we go outside and throw the newspaper into the wormhole? I think by now the other councilors will be waiting."

Enela was on the verge of panic. She did not know what Ari-Ana was up to, but she had a certain sensation that it was not good. Then she had an idea. Not a very good idea, but at this stage anything would be better than nothing.

"Arina, Hila," she called out, "take a look at this and make sure it's the right paper."

The other two moved to look over Enela's shoulder as she thumbed through the paper. They agreed that the paper looked like the one they had seen on Wednesday. Except for the advertising section that is. Both were certain there was no advertising section in the paper they had seen on Wednesday.

"Let's make this a valuable souvenir," Enela suggested. "We can each sign it …"

With that, Enela picked up the pencil she had been using to do some of the math calculations and wrote her name in some white space on a furniture ad. Then she handed the pencil to each of the others who also wrote their names beside hers. Enela felt that the signatures would somehow fit in with Ari-Ana's plan. Indeed, Ari-Ana made no effort to stop them.

But Ari-Ana had grown impatient with the delays. Finally she said, "Shall we go outside now. That wormhole won't last forever."

The four of them made their way out of the control room and outside the cave to the waiting wormhole. There were several councilors waiting for them. They were marveling at the wormhole shimmering in the sunlight. Ari-Ana greeted them and told them that they were about to send a copy of today's newspaper back in time to last Wednesday when, as she had previously reported, Enela had found it and brought it to her attention. She even mentioned that Enela, Arina and Hila had signed the paper. As she was talking, she retrieved the paper from Enela and held it up so all could see it.

Before she had quite finished her speech, Enela, who had been silently counting off the seconds left in the wormhole's lifetime, interrupted her.

"Ari-Ana, the wormhole is about to collapse. We have to throw the newspaper – now!" She quickly grabbed the newspaper from Ari-Ana and quickly thrust it into the wormhole. In the process, the advertising insert slipped out of the paper and fell to the ground - outside the wormhole.

Ari-Ana did her best to grab the advertising insert and toss it into the wormhole as well, but just at that point the wormhole gave its characteristic pop and disappeared from view.

Ari-Ana just stood there for a minute or more as though she was in shock. Then she turned and almost glared at Enela. The other councilors intervened at this point and announced that there would be a closed Council session on Monday. Ari-Ana was to bring the newspaper and Enela, Arina and Hila were to be present as well in case there were any questions. With that Ari-Ana and the other councilors moved swiftly back toward the Valley.

"What was that all about?" asked Arina.

"I don't know," Enela answered. "Something's going on. I don't know what it is, but Ari-Ana wanted to ensure that what went through the wormhole today was nothing like what I found. For some reason she does not want the others to accept that we can really travel back in time."

"But why?" from Hila. To that question there was no answer.

The three went back to the control room, shut off the power and closed the ship as they left. Then they went back to the Valley to relax for a while.

The three sought out a toilet, some food and water and then retired to the supply bunker to talk over what they had heard and seen. Enela's mind wasn't quite on topic; she was thinking about her meeting with Mary on Sunday.

Sunday dawned bright and promising. Enela, Arina and Hila met early and laid out the steps for the next series of tests. After some discussion it was agreed that Hila would secure some reptiles and birds, Arina would gather the insects and arachnids, and Enela would be responsible for the mammals. The other two had great mental images of Enela scampering around the desert trying to capture a rabbit or a coyote. Then they each set off on their respective endeavors.

The first thing Enela did was head off to Gray Wolf's cabin. There she persuaded him to get Sheriff Billy Eagle to round up a few of the strays that were always wandering around the reservation. She said she would come by and pick them up in a couple of days. She also had to promise that they would not suffer any harm and would be turned loose again as soon as they had served their purpose. She was just a little vague as to what that purpose really was. In the end Gray Wolf agreed.

Then Enela headed back to the cliff dwellings where she was to meet Mary. She scampered up the rockslide below the opening to the cave and worked her way around to the first level of the dwellings. She had a while to wait. Then at last she could see a plume of dust off toward Winton and knew it had to be Mary.

Mary stopped in the parking area near the riverbed and walked over to the cliff face carrying a large picnic basket and a blanket. Enela lowered the climbing log and helped Mary tote the goodies up to the ledge. They took up residence in one of the rooms. Mary spread the blanket out and they sat down.

The afternoon was spent engaging in much small talk about everything and nothing. Mary kept offering food and drink from the basket she had brought. While it was all wonderfully appropriate human food, Enela could only take in the smallest nibbles of cheese and chicken. Her body simply had no way of processing vegetable material, and there was no way for any excess to come out except the way it went in.

Enela finally convinced Mary that this was a physiological problem and had nothing to do with the quality of Mary's cooking. In comforting her hurt feelings, Enela had reached out to touch Mary's arm. This closeness had resulted in a very pleasant sensation. Mary didn't protest when Enela slowly moved her hand up to Mary's shoulder, and then to her back. Mary moved closer and rested her hand on Enela's leg. Enela had not felt such sensations since the night back in the hospital. At that time she had relegated those sensations to a dream. Now they were very real.

The two moved even closer, embracing each other. Enela was unabashedly stroking Mary's back. Mary paused for a moment, then kissed Enela, first on the forehead then quite passionately on the mouth.

"You're always running around out here like a nudist," she said. "I feel decidedly over dressed." And with that she pulled off her t-shirt, unfastened her jeans and pulled them down, losing her shoes in the process. Then she put her arms back around Enela and pulled her down to the blanket.

Enela had never felt human skin so intimately. She gently stroked Mary's arms and back. Mary repaid the favor, caressing Enela's back and legs. Pure passion was rapidly taking over from any remaining vestige of reason. Enela had never had the opportunity to investigate a human so closely, she was moving her hands all over Mary's body, exploring her hair, her breasts, running her hand inside Mary's panties to explore the wet spot between her legs.

Mary managed to remove her bra and Enela tugged her panties off, marveling at the curly hair exposed beneath them. The two lay entwined on the blanket, each passionately stroking and kissing the other. Mary was by now very wet and responding with spasms to Enela's every touch, but Enela's crotch remained stubbornly unmoved by the touch.

"What do I do to turn you on?" Mary finally gasped in desperation.

"You mustn't," Enela whispered. The two continued to lie together for some time.

"Oh, my gosh," Mary said when she saw the time, "I've got to get out of here while I can still see the track through the sand." She got up, rummaged in her purse for a brush and did her best to straighten out her mussed hair.

"I don't have to worry about things like that," Enela piped up. Mary threw the brush at her. As Mary was putting on her bra and panties, Enela repeated her previous comment. The two were suddenly locked into a tight embrace, until Mary finally broke free, saying "I really have to go!"

****

Ron Baker was a photo interpreter working for the US government's super secret intelligence organization known as the National Reconnaissance Office. In the past they had been one of the primary sources for intelligence gleaned from covert satellite imaging. They usually spied on other countries, but since the 9/11 tragedy they had assumed a new role – looking for possible problems within the United States. Ron was part of that effort.

In the old days satellite imagery had to be dropped by parachute in special canisters which were then collected by aircraft, hopefully before they hit the ground or water. Now, images were sent down electronically. The satellites could stay up much longer and cover much more ground. Ron had designed a special computer program which would automatically compare two satellite passes over the same area and warn of any significant changes. This greatly reduced the time that headquarters' analysts had to spend on routine images and speeded the image's arrival at ancillary agencies which did the detail work.

Ron was enjoying a quiet shift until that alarm went off. He called up the suspect frames and took a look. A plot of the images told him that the area being covered was out in Arizona. What, he wondered, could possibly be happening out in the desert.

The computer advised him that the potential problem was a suspect excavation. Ron examined the images. He could see what looked to be a large hole in the side of a butte. The hole was in the shade. He could not see how deep it was or what might be inside it. He looked at the rock fall beneath the hole. It did look a little larger, as though part of the upper wall had been removed.

A hole of this sort would not, in and of itself, be a matter of concern. But this was close to the border and in a relatively desolate area of the state. Ron made a copy of the images and saved them for future research. Then he released the transmission for routine processing.

Ron mentally flipped a coin. 9/11 was still a fresh memory. It probably wouldn't hurt to check. Besides, Washington agencies were supposed to be sharing information – the latest memo had said so. He reached for his phone book, dialed a local number and asked for a contact in Tucson. It would do the FBI good to get out in the field for a day.

Ron used a secure phone to brief the Tucson FBI office station chief on the problem. He was able to pass them the exact coordinates of the suspect hole and even send them a copy of the image. There were no agents immediately available, but the chief assured him that they would get an agent out there within a week – or so.

Chapter 11

The Plan

When Arina, Hila and Enela met on Monday to continue their experiments with the wormhole, Arina and Hila were impressed with how well Enela looked. 'Bright and sparkly' were Arina's words. Enela just pooh-poohed the whole thing and set about fashioning a wormhole for their tests.

They had brought some short range radios from the supply bunker so that they could coordinate their efforts. It was agreed that Enela would stay inside the ship and establish the wormholes. Arina and Hila would stay outside and run the tests. One of them would release an animal into the wormhole while the other waited at the output point to catch the animal. They wanted to keep the animals for a short period to check for any delayed effects.

The first tests involved several beetles, two tarantulas and a scorpion. All passed through the wormhole without any obvious ill effects. In fact one beetle came out of the wormhole and immediately spread its wings and flew off before "Hila could catch it.

The second round involved a Gila monster, a horned toad and a couple of non-descript lizards. They also passed through the wormhole with no problems. After all of the small animals had been tested, some more than once, Hila and Arina came inside the ship to ask Enela about her mammals.

"I have them on order," she explained. "But right now let's go tell Ari-Ula what we have found. I have to go back for my next session with Red Hawk."

"How much longer are these sessions with Red Hawk going to last?" Arina asked.

"I don't know," Enela sighed. "Can't be much longer if we're all going to be leaving here." Enela stopped on that thought. It was suddenly very depressing.

It was shortly after noon when Ari-Ula convened the Council. Enela, Arina and Hila sat along the side of the room and waited for their services to be required. The first item on the agenda was the newspaper. Ari-Ana produced the copy she had been preserving since last Wednesday for all of the Council members to examine. The main question in everyone's mind - was this the same paper that they had seen tossed into the wormhole? How could they be sure?

Ari-Ana told them about the signatures in the furniture ad. They started thumbing through the paper looking for the ad. But they could not find the ad. This caught Enela's attention.

"Wait a minute!" she exclaimed, jumping to her feet. "We signed the paper before we threw it into the wormhole." She ran over to the Council table to see for herself. Sure enough, there was no ad, and there were no signatures. Before the Councilors could react and remind her to remember her place, Enela was at it again. "That's not the same paper!"

"But, Enela," Ari-Ana was confidently smooth, "I showed you the paper Saturday morning and you even commented on how new it

142

was. This paper is just as new." The Councilors were beginning to nod in agreement.

"But the paper I found in the desert was *not* new! This is not the same paper I gave you on Wednesday!" Enela was becoming defiant again. But besides attracting the displeasure of the Councilors she had attracted the attention of Arina and Hila. They came up to the Council table to join her and examine the newspaper. In a heartbeat they agreed that the newspaper laying on the table was definitely not the one they had seen on Wednesday. It was far too fresh and new. To emphasize her claim Enela rubbed her fingers over the page, smearing the ink.

"The ink is still fresh," she pointed out. "The ink would certainly have dried on a paper that had been laying around for over three days."

This caught everyone's attention. The other councilors looked at Ari-Ana with something more than a question in their eyes.

"Well, Ari-Ana, how do you answer that? The ink would not smear as readily in an older paper." There was no accusation in Ari-Ula's voice, but the question clearly demanded an answer. Ari-Ana looked very uncomfortable.

"Very well," she answered. "That is not the original paper. I asked Red Hawk to bring me two papers Saturday morning. The one with the signatures that we threw through the wormhole and this one. I wanted to make you sufficiently unsure of the wormhole's capability that you would cancel the Plan."

"But why would you do that?" asked one of the Councilors. "You were as eager as everyone else to engage the Plan."

"Yes, I was," Ari-Ana responded. "But, since we conceived the Plan, I have been privy to additional information which now makes me doubt whether the Plan will work at all."

"What information? And why weren't we told?" Ari-Ula was incredulous. "Ari-Ana this is not within your purview as a junior councilor. First, bring us the original newspaper, if you still have it. The I want a full explanation of your actions."

Ari-Ana left the Council chambers to retrieve the newspaper. Enela, Arina and Hila were sent back to the sidelines and the Councilors put their heads together and conferred quietly among themselves.

When Ari-Ana returned, she brought with her the original newspaper. Again, everyone gathered to examine it. This time the paper showed its age. But there were still no signatures. Ari-Ana provided the solution. She had also brought along the advertising supplement that had fallen out of the paper as it was tossed into the wormhole. There, on page two, were the signatures.

"So, Ari-Ana," said Ari-Ula, "suppose you tell us why you are now so determined that the Plan will not work."

"I can not," Ari-Ana answered with some difficulty. "I have been privileged to learn some things which cast great doubt on the Plan. I am not in a position to divulge what I have learned nor the source of the information. If what I have learned is true, then there is no hope that the Plan will have the desired result. It could, in fact, be a total disaster and even cause the destruction of all

144

our people. Perhaps in another week or two I will have enough information to explain the problem."

"You ask us to accept the unproven statements of a person who has already proven duplicitous? You ask us to wait for an unspecified period and then do not promise proof positive?" Ari-Ula was visibly upset. She had sponsored Ari-Ana for her seat on the Council. She was sure her judgment had been correct, but she was having great difficulty justifying it after the behavior she had just witnessed.

"Ari-Ana," she said at last, "you will retire from the Council meeting. We will consider what you have said and what you have done. I will confer with you later."

Ari-Ana bowed to the Council and left the chamber. Enela, Arina and Hila also got up and started to leave the chamber. They were clearly no longer needed. But Enela hesitated, then she walked back to the Council table. The other two stopped and waited to see what new catastrophe she was about to initiate.

When Enela reached the dais, she bowed and gave it her best shot. "Ari-Ula, since we seem to have been so intimately involved, would it be possible for us to be told about 'The Plan'?"

Ari-Ula looked a bit perturbed. Then her demeanor softened. "Until now, the Plan has been held in great secrecy. Only the Councilors were aware of it. It came about when you first discovered the spaceship in the cave. We will soon be telling everyone, so there is no reason that you should not have the privilege of hearing about it first.

"As you probably know we live here as castaways, exiles from our people, and under the constant threat of being discovered by the humans who populate this world. It has been our single most pressing desire to reunite the Elders on this planet with those from our home world. We first thought that we might be able to use the spaceship to travel in search of them. That first plan was dashed when you discovered that it was far too small and that it was not operable.

"The revised plan involved using the time-travel potential of the wormhole to return to Elderhome prior to the exodus. For this plan to work we had to secure the exact location of Elderhome and be sure that the wormhole could indeed move objects back in time.

"Ari-Sona accomplished the first objective by studying the star system displays at night while you were resting. She found one that matched the display on the cave wall. The navigation system kindly provided the necessary coordinates. We ere going to have you validate them just before we formally announced the Plan.

"The newspaper was the key element in the second objective. Now that we know time travel is possible, we still have to demonstrate that we can travel through the wormhole without injury. If that can be proven, we will execute the Plan.

"Now it is essential that you continue your work with the wormhole generator. You must continue your tests with living creatures: insects, reptiles, small mammals. If they are successful, completely successful, then we will have to try sending a volunteer through. In the future, please report directly to me. Ari-Ula was very pleased with their progress. She thanked the three for their dedication and urged them to finish the tests as soon as possible. You can go now, but please, for the moment, tell no one about the Plan."

When she had dismissed them, Arina and Hila left the Councilors still conferring in an animated state. They themselves were in a state of shock after hearing the details of the Plan. There had always been talk about rejoining the others from the home world. But it had been just that – talk. Now the Councilors were actually considering a means to actually carry out such a plan. And Ari-Ana had been against it. Why? What did she know that she wasn't willing to talk about?

Enela went over to a side room where Red Hawk was waiting for her, deep in meditation as usual. Enela sat down opposite Red Hawk and waited patiently to be recognized.

"Good afternoon, Enela," Red Hawk said, without any apparent change in her demeanor. "Do you have any questions for me today?"

"Nothing very philosophical, I'm afraid," Enela answered. "But … well, this whole process was Ari-Ana's idea, and after the last Council meeting … well, I was just wondering … "

"What's to come of our sessions and how much longer they will last? And, perhaps, to whom I am now reporting?"

"Yeah, something like that."

"I am going to have a long talk with Ari-Ula," Red Hawk explained. "She wants to know just what was going on. I understand that Ari-Ana did not confide in her. I will give her a summary of the more salient things that I have learned to date."

"I am not crazy!", Enela interrupted.

"I know you are not, Enela," Red Hawk was reassuring. "But you are unique among the Elders, for two reasons. First, you were raised by humans through most of your developmental years. You did not have the normal Elder upbringing and training. For this reason you often react in ways that are not embraced by the Elders, but are perfectly normal from your unique point of view. This tends to surprise them and make them feel uneasy that they cannot predict your behavior. This is something they are learning, very slowly, to live with.

"The second reason is even more surprising. Your race memory clearly extends much further back than does that of most Elders in the Valley."

At this statement, Enela looked up sharply with a sudden renewed interest in what Red Hawk was saying. "You mean that I can remember things that happened when we first arrived on this planet?"

"That and more," continued Red Hawk. "In fact, it was your memories that prompted Ari-Ana to try to cancel the Plan. She wants to use the wormhole for something else entirely."

"Why? What did I remember?"

"That you will have to determine for yourself. They are your memories. I only have some bits and pieces of them. That is the problem that Ari-Ana was faced with. I could not tell her how all the images I saw actually fit together, or in exactly what order they occurred.

"This may well be our last session. I would like to find out, in so far as we can manage, what really happened when the Elders ended up here. Are you ready to begin?"

Enela did her best to quiet her racing mind and to enter into a deep trance. Before it had always been something akin to serious boredom, this time it was more like falling asleep. Her mind would try to shut down, then wake long enough to flirt with some fleeting idea, and then shut down again. Finally, all of the odd ideas faded away into blackness.

When she came back to outward consciousness she saw Red Hawk sitting opposite her. Red Hawk was neither smiling nor frowning. It looked as though she was pondering some serious problem. As soon as she ascertained that Enela had come completely out of the trance, she dismissed her without any further comment.

Enela wandered about the Valley for a bit, then she tended to her body's needs and returned to the supply bunker to sleep. But sleep did not come easily; she had far too much to think about.

The next day Enela, Arina and Hila went back to the cave to check on the results of the previous day's experiments. Arina had brought food along for the animals and doled it out as she checked each subject. All of their test subjects seemed to be in fine condition.

As soon as they had determined that all was well, Hila brought up their need for mammalian test subjects and she and Arina turned to Enela for her response.

"I didn't expect that we would be ready for mammals so soon," she replied nonchalantly, "but let's go see!" She led them back to Gray Wolf's cabin. When they arrived Gray Wolf was nowhere to be found, but there were two dogs tied up next to the cabin and a strange burro in the corral. Enela couldn't help laughing at Arina's and Hila's quizzical expressions.

"I asked Gray Wolf the other day if he and Sheriff Billy could round up some strays for us," she explained. "These must be what they have found. Let's take them back to the cave and set up a wormhole."

The burro came along willingly, but the dogs had no intention of being led around on a leash. After a couple of near bites and a lot of serious growling, Hila finally managed to calm them.

"Oh, dear," Enela commented. "I do hope you haven't ruined their ability run loose. I did promise Gray Wolf that we wouldn't harm any of the animals he collected."

"Not at all," answered Hila. "I just strongly suggested to them that had better respect us or we would tear them limb from limb. Or whatever the equivalent is in dog terms. I think they got the big picture that we are the alpha males around here, not them." Enela and Arina were suitably impressed.

As they left, Enela scooped up one of the chickens pecking around in front of the cabin. "We haven't tried a bird," was her reply to the curious looks of the others.

The tests didn't take long and all went quite well. Hila shooed the dogs through the wormhole one at a time, then both together. She left the leases attached so that Arina and Enela had no real trouble catching them again at the other end. The burro also made an uneventful trip through the wormhole. Then Hila got a brilliant idea. She lined up the burro for another trip and placed one of the dogs on its back. The burro had no intention of going through again, but a sharp whack on its rear persuaded it to go through. When it emerged at the other end the dog was still on its back. Both appeared quite healthy.

The chicken had no intention of walking into the wormhole, encouragement or not. Hila finally picked it up and tossed it gently into the wormhole. The chicken came out the other side flapping its wings with great abandon and flopping down in the sand in a most undignified manner. It promptly stood up, shook itself off and started strutting around as though nothing at all unusual had happened. Enela and Arina almost doubled over laughing.

They returned the animals to Gray Wolf's cabin, provided them with food and water and left a note of thanks for Gray Wolf. They were about to return to the Valley to report their progress to Ari-Ula, but Arina held back a bit, as though she had something on her mind.

"What's up?" Hila asked.

"I was just thinking that we probably ought to run one more test before we go back to Ari-Ula," Arina said.

"What kind of test?" Enela regretted asking the question as soon as it was out of her mouth.

"Well, the animals seem to have survived. I was just wondering what it would feel like to go through the wormhole."

"What? Us?" Hila was not at all sure she liked that idea.

"Well," Arina said, "that is what it's all about. All of these tests are just to determine if it's safe for us to go through. Besides, the aliens must have done it quite routinely."

"Yes," Enela was siding with Hila on this one, "but they did it inside a spaceship. We aren't the aliens, and we certainly won't be able to make the trip in a spaceship. We don't even know if there are any delayed affects. It has only been a few hours since we started the tests. What about some lingering affect on our eggs or sperm?"

"A day is a long time in the life of an insect or spider," was Arina's answer. "They seem to be doing quite well. I'm sure that the aliens wouldn't have used a wormhole if it caused them any genetic problems. As for us, we'll never know unless we try. I'm willing to have a go at it, if you'll set up a wormhole, Enela."

They spent some time discussing the pro's and con's of such a test. But neither Hila nor Enela could dampen Arina's enthusiasm. In the end they determined that Arina wasn't pregnant and was reasonably healthy. Enela agreed to set up a wormhole, a very short wormhole, for one test.

When the wormhole was established the three went down to the desert floor together. Hila went to the end of the wormhole while Enela waited with Arina.

"Are you sure you want to do this?" Enela asked. She considered trying to talk Arina out of it, if she was anything she was considerably over eager. But Arina was still excited about the prospect of wormhole travel and would have none of it. Then with a parting smile, Arina stepped smartly into the mouth of the wormhole and disappeared.

Enela raced quickly to the other end of the wormhole. At first nothing was visible. Then as she got to the far end she saw Hila standing there gaping backward into the wormhole exit. Just as she came up, the wormhole expired with its usual soft pop and Enela could see Arina standing there with a huge smile and a look of absolute ecstasy on her face.

"Arina!" she exclaimed, "What happened? How do you feel? How was it?!"

"Wow!" was Arina's only answer for a couple of minutes. Then she continued, "It was a rush! Quite cold and dark, but just for an instant. I had the feeling that I was traveling at a tremendous speed, but there was no wind or tumbling. I just stepped into the wormhole and then continued the same step out of it. I don't know if I'm still fertile, but my mind seems to be in working order and all of my muscles are still responding and my heart is still beating. Oh, I want to set up one of these at a carnival! We could make a fortune!"

"Well, I guess we have something to tell Ari-Ula now," Hila said, beaming at their success.

"Yes, we had better tell her," Enela agreed, but let's keep an eye on Arina and the other animals for a day or so, just in case."

Ari-Ula was quite happy with the results of the animal tests, but less satisfied with Arina's own test. Yet, even she had to admit that such a test would have ultimately been necessary. She asked the three to stay at the Council chamber while she summoned the other Councilors.

Once they were all assembled, except for Ari-Ana – who was still under suspension, Ari-Ula relayed the results of the tests to the others, including Arina's trip through the wormhole. They were all suitably impressed. A few of the Councilors even asked questions as to how the tests were done and how the various animals were being monitored. They seemed satisfied with the answers. They were especially interested in what Arina had experienced.

"It now comes to the question of implementing the Plan," Ari-Ula said. "We have completed all of the prerequisites. It is now time for a final decision. That decision must be unanimous. What shall we do?"

The Councilors became quiet and each had the appearance of going into deep meditation. The chamber became eerily still. They remained in that state for several minutes. Then, as quickly as they had entered the trance, they came out of it and Ari-Ula said, "It is decided. All Elders will be summoned to return to the Valley within a month. Ari-Ula then turned to Enela, Arina and Hila. "You will all monitor the test subjects carefully for any sign of potential damage.

"Arina, you will carefully monitor your health and immediately report any potential problems. Take no unnecessary risks for the next week or so, just in case.

"Enela, you and Ari-Sona will work out the proper coordinates to prepare a wormhole to transport the Elders to Elderhome."

Ari-Ula then dismissed everyone, asking Enela to remain behind for a few minutes. Once they were alone, Ari-Ula said, "Enela, I have a special task for you. Once we have left here, we will have no further use for that spaceship. I fear what might happen if the humans on this planet find out about it. I want you to find a way to destroy it after we have all departed. If there is no built-in destruction procedure, perhaps you can find a way to overload one of the power cells, or something. If all else fails we can always just load it with explosives. Let me know if you need anything. You may go now … And do not talk about this to anyone, is that understood?"

"Yes, Ari-Ula," Enela replied and left the Council chamber, thinking about what Ari-Ula had said. She did not yet know just how prophetic Ari-Ula's comments would be.

Chapter 12

Saving the Past

Enela returned the her favorite hangout – the supply bunker. When she entered, she heard the voice of Ari-Ana from a back corner. Enela hastened toward the sound.

"Ari-Ana," Enela almost stuttered, "How can I help you?"

"I do need your help, Enela," Ari-Ana began. "I am afraid I acted to prematurely, when I pulled the newspaper stunt. I didn't have the information I needed to follow up when it fizzled. I just received the last details from Red Hawk and they prove I was right. But they are too late to help me now. Ari-Ula and I are not on very good terms at the moment.

"As awkward as it seems, I really need you to act as an intermediary between Ari-Ula and myself until we can get matters straightened out."

"How do I do that?" Enela asked with some trepidation. She definitely did not like the way this conversation was headed.

"Just this," Ari-Ana reassured her. "I need you to search your memory for everything that happened when we first arrived on this world." When you are personally aware of all the details, you will know what to do." Then Ari-Ana added, "I know this will be difficult, but I also know that you can do it . And it is imperative that you *do* do it."

With that, Ari-Ana left the supply bunker. Enela just stood there in shock, too stunned to even ponder what Ari-Ana had said.

Eventually, the shock wore off. Ari-Ana had said that it was imperative for her to remember the past, so Enela decided that she had better get at it. She found a comfortable spot and sat down. Recalling past memories took diligence and some persistence. Enela had occasionally searched her memory for past knowledge, but never so far back – and for what? What was she supposed to find?

There was nothing to do but try. Enela sat back and started focusing her memory on the past. It would help if she had some idea of the subject matter she was searching for. Just searching 'the past' was far too vague.

Enela paused to think. Ari-Ana was concerned about using the worm hole generator. But that was working well. It couldn't be the problem. The alien ship itself! Where had it come from? And why? Enela focused on the ship. It was slow work at first. There were too many little bits and pieces. At first Enela just made a note of each one and moved on. When she could find no more, she went back and tried to put them in order.

The bits and pieces weren't numbered and couldn't be sorted. She just had to arrange them into some sort of coherent picture. It took time and it was terribly difficult and stressful. After several hours at it, a coherent picture did begin to emerge.

The alien ship was expected. It arrived with a crew of five, all fully armed. There was a plan to defeat the aliens. It had come from … Wait a minute, something is wrong. Enela refocused on the Elders. A group of six had arrived on a lifeboat. But, to defeat the aliens required many more. Where did these extra Elders come from. Was there a second ship? No, no second ship. Then where? Were they already on Earth? Of course, that had to be it.

Enela was getting confused and tired. She started going around in circles. There was no beginning and no end. She just went around and around. Elders coming from space. Elders on Earth. But the Elders on Earth didn't come from space. They were already here. But the Elders came from space.

Suddenly, it all came together. Where did the Elders who were already here come from? From here! It was so simple; why hadn't she seen it. The Elders who arrived on the lifeboat were too few and unarmed. They had no chance of defeating the aliens by themselves. If they didn't defeat the aliens, then there would be no Elders on Earth. But the Elders were here, dating by all estimates from that first lifeboat. And, by all estimates, from an initial group of fifteen or sixteen!

"Bingo!" Enela thought to herself. That was what Ari-Ana had discovered. Unless we send a group of armed Elders back to the original arrival point, the ones that came on the lifeboat won't survive to produce us. The ship we discovered in the cave must be that original alien ship.

Then a more modern memory interrupted Enela's thought. The two extra weapons in the locker! They must be the ones we sent back to the past with our Elders. Or, will send back to the past. Enela's mind was beginning to reel again.

"Never mind the paradox," she thought. "I have to get this information to Ari-Ula!"

Enela struggled to her feet, stretched, and headed to the entrance to the supply bunker. As she approached the entrance, the darkness of the bunker gave way to light. It was already morning. She went directly to the Council chamber.

When Enela entered the chamber, she saw Ari-Sona at the dais. "Excuse, me." Enela said, and bowed to Ari-Sona, "May I speak to Ari-Ula."

"Of course," Ari-Sona replied. "I will summon her."

In a few minutes, Ari-Ula appeared and greeted Enela. "Good morning, Enela, have you some news?"

"I do, Ari-Ula", Enela said as she bowed respectfully. "As you know, Ari-Ana and Red Hawk have been examining my memories of our past. When Ari-Ana spoke of a 'problem' the other day, she was referring to a part of what she had learned. Last night I managed to trace those memories. I now know exactly what the 'problem' is. I can relate it to you, if you are interested."

"Ari-Ana told me she was attempting to get at the root of your problem adjusting to our community." Ari-Ula was not yet accusing anyone of anything, but she was at the brink. Is this the 'problem' you are referring to?"

"No, Ari-Ula. The problem I am referring to involves the worm hole generator and our history on this planet."

"Oh?" Ari-Ula seemed truly interested, "Tell me more."

Enela related what she had learned from her memory probe. She couldn't explain all the whys and wherefores, but her story was convincing. When Enela had finished, Ari-Ula paused for several seconds before responding.

"Whether it makes much sense or not," Ari-Ula finally said. "it looks like we have some work to do.

"The first step will be to send a few volunteers back to our point of arrival on this planet to ensure that all goes well. Then all of the Elders who have been summoned back to the Valley will make the journey back to Elderhome as planned."

Ari-Ula turned to Ari-Sona, "Summon the councilors and Hila," she ordered.

When all were in attendance, Ari-Ula informed them of what she had learned. There was a brief discussion of the new information. The consensus was that the Council should order the relief of the original Elders, since apparently they had already done so. Ari-Ula made the pronouncement.

"Hila, select a team of ten and make preparations to depart within a week. You will have to take with you anything that you suspect you may need. Enela, prepare the coordinates for their travel back to our initial arrival. If you have any new information to offer along the way, bring it to my attention immediately."

Enela and Hila were then excused to make their preparations.

When they had departed, Ari-Ula turned her attention to Ari-Ana. "I presume," Ari-Ula said, "that Enela's revelation came at your instigation. Would you care to add anything?"

Ari-Ana was now backed into a corner. "Yes, it did," she admitted. "When you first proposed what has been called 'The Plan', I had my doubts; but I had no basis for them – just a gut feeling. You know I had a project underway to research our roots here on this planet. I was having trouble finding anyone whose memory went all the way back to our beginning.

"When Enela came to us, I included her in the project. I felt that I might learn something about what made her so different from all the rest. When my efforts failed, I enlisted the aid of Red Hawk. She had worked with Enela previously and I hoped that the bond she built then might aid her in probing Enela's memory.

"We were actually proceeding nicely, in bits and pieces, I could actually see the end coming, but we weren't there yet when the newspaper incident occurred. I was afraid that exposing the process at that point would foul up everything. Once I was censored, I asked Enela to finish the job for me. I have done all that I can alone; I will now go back to my quarters." With that, Ari-Ana turned and started to leave the dais.

"Wait, Ari-Ana," Ari-Ula called after her. "I am afraid I acted far too rashly. I apologize to you and to the other Councilors for my reaction. Won't you please join us again? We have much work to do."

* * * * * * * * * * * * * * * * * * * *

That afternoon, Sheriff Billy Eagle had a surprise visitor in his Wakulla office. He introduced himself as Robert Askins, special agent from the FBI field office in Tucson.

"So, what brings you all the way out to Wakulla?" Billy asked. "Come to see our show?"

"No, not really," Agent Askins answered. "Although I understand it's a real crowd pleaser. No, I've been asked to look into a little excavation that is going on out here on the reservation. I'm sure it's really nothing, but being this close to the border, it's got some folks curious."

"Excavation?" Billy was curious, too. "I don't know of any excavations going on around here. Could you be a little more specific?"

"I'm sorry," Askins said. "I don't mean to sound mysterious. I can't reveal my sources, but I have been asked to take a look around these coordinates." He handed Billy a piece of paper with the coordinates on it. "I was hoping you could help me locate the place."

Billy took one look and then went to a file cabinet and pulled out a map of the reservation. He spread it out on his desk and proceeded to locate the spot. It was close to the Valley, but far enough away to be reasonably safe.

"You said you were looking for an 'excavation'. Can *you* be a bit more specific?" Billy really wanted to know what was going on without seeming too pushy.

"It is supposed to be a large hole in the side of a butte. Do you, perhaps, know the place?" Askins sounded a little bored. Billy didn't think he was hiding   anything meaningful.

"I know the butte," Billy admitted. "It's next to a dry river bed and houses some old Indian pueblos. I don't know of any excavations or holes in the vicinity. I'll be glad to take you there, if you like. There aren't any roads out to the butte, you'll have to travel across bare sand."

"I have a GPS locator with me," Askins said, "and my SUV has 4-wheel drive; but I'm no great talent at driving across the desert. I'll take you up on the offer."

"Give me a moment to tell my staff where I'll be," Billy said. "Then I'll lead you out there in my Jeep." He was quick to add, "Just in case I get called back for an emergency. I'm virtually the only law enforcement for the reservation."

Billy went into the back room and closed the door. Agent Askins could hear him talking on the radio, but the words were too muffled for him to make out exactly what was being said. He did not, however, detect anything out of the norm.

Billy led the way out of Wakulla, heading west into the desert toward the butte. He deliberately took the long way around, eventually approaching the butte from the south. Billy knew he was testing the SUV's ability, 4-wheel drive or not. If Agent Askins noted anything suspicious, he remained quite silent. It was late in the afternoon when they approached the site. Billy stopped in the parking area southwest of the butte.

"We had better walk from here," he said. "The community college comes out here to use the area as a dig site, so this area is pretty well tamped down. The other side is still very much loose sand."

Askins wasn't about to argue. He was still bouncing around from the rough ride.

They walked around the butte to the eastern side. Askins was checking his GPS unit. It indicated that he was at the right place. They were standing at the base of a large rockslide. Looking up there was no indication of a hole.

"Well," Billy asked, "is this the right place? I don't see any indication of an 'excavation'."

"This is the spot," Askins agreed. He peered intently up toward the top of the butte. "I think I may see something up there. I'm going to climb up and take a look."

"That may not be safe. Those rocks don't look too secure." Billy sounded truly worried. But Askins wasn't about to be deterred. He started climbing, very carefully, up the rocks.

Billy watched him work his way up. He could only hope that his message had made it to its intended recipient and that he had understood. Askins was now almost three fourths the way up. He stopped.

"There is a hole here!" he shouted down. "A big one! I'm going to have a look inside." Suddenly there was a bright flash near the top of the butte. Askins seemed to crumple. His body slipped some distance down the rocks and lay still.

"You brought us a live one this time," Gray Wolf had come up behind Billy while he was watching the butte. "You can go on back to Wakulla. We'll deal with him."

"Gray Wolf, you can't mess around with this guy like he's some roving college student. He's

164

FBI. If anything happens to him there will be big trouble. I'm sure he reported that I was with him when we came out here."

"Don't worry," Gray Wolf assured Billy. "We have never failed you yet. We will handle it. You may have to answer some questions, but just deny everything and all will be well. Now go on back to town and have a good evening."

Billy was still muttering under his breath as he drove back to Wakulla.

* * * * * * * * * * * * * * * * * *

Gray Wolf had been at his cabin when Billy Eagle's radio call came through. He immediately had gone to the Valley to tell the Councilors about the potential problem. Their great fear was that the government had learned, or was about to learn, about the spacecraft.

Ari-Ula had not seen Enela since she had last spoken to her. She presumed that she would still be at the spacecraft, working on her latest assignment. She asked Gray Wolf to accompany her back to the butte. Even as they arrived they could see a small cloud of dust in the direction of Wakulla.

"Gray Wolf," Ari-Ula cautioned, "please wait here at the north end of the butte in case we need your help. If all goes well, just send Billy back to Wakulla. The less he knows about what is going on out here the better."

Gray Wolf gave an uncharacteristic mutter that *he* didn't know much about what was going on at the butte. But he waited patiently at the edge of the butte as Ari-Ula quickly scaled the rocks to the cave.

Ari-Ula breathed a sigh of relief when she got to the cave and saw that the ship was still standing open. That meant that Enela was working inside. Ari-Ula hurried up the gangway and up to the control room.

"Enela," she said on entering the control room, "we are about to have some unwelcome visitors. Is there anything we can do to stop them or to seal the cave? Now!"

Enela was startled by the sudden appearance of Ari-Ula. Her question only added to the confusion. "Visitors?" she responded. "How many? How soon? Who?"

Ari-Ula's answers were crisp and to the point. "FBI. One or two. In about ten minutes."

"There's no way we can close the cave," Enela answered. "That would take explosives and might damage the ship. At any rate it would set the Plan back at least two or three weeks while we dug it all out again.

"If we can climb the rocks, so can they," Ari-Ula observed. "Since we enlarged the opening to let in more light any human can get through it. Our only chance is to stop them. Preferably without killing them ..." Ari-Ula added.

The sound of the cars arriving on the other side of the butte was clearly audible. Enela thought wildly about setting up a wormhole. But to do it accurately would take some time – and it would give away the very thing they were trying to protect. She had a momentary vision of several large black helicopters swooping out of the sky to unload their cargo of armed special forces troops. If the humans learned of the ship and the Elders it would mean the end of her people. They would either be scattered or killed. They had no weapons – they wouldn't stand a chance …

"Wait," Enela said. "Weapons! We have the aliens' weapons. We can use one of them!"

"I really don't want to disintegrate anybody," Ari-Ula was getting a weird mental image of roasted or disappearing bodies.

"We tried one once on a cactus," Enela explained. "On the lowest setting it didn't seem to do too much damage. Besides, it the only option we have."

She rushed to the weapons locker, took out one of the fully charged hand weapons and set it to the lowest setting. Then, reconsidering her options, she upped it by one notch.

The two rushed out of the ship and over to the edge of the cave opening. Just as they arrived they could see someone climbing up the rocks below them. He was almost to the mouth of the cave. He stopped and yelled back to the person on the ground that he had found the opening. At just that moment, Enela aimed the weapon at him and fired it. The human crumpled down into the rocks and lay still.

At that moment Gray Wolf came out of the shadows and spoke to the person at the base of the rocks. He was telling Sheriff Billy to go back to town and let the Elders clean up the mess. Billy hesitated at first; then he turned and headed back to his Jeep. When he had left, Ari-Ula and Enela went down to the body to ascertain if it was still alive.

There didn't seem to be any outward damage, but Enela wasn't sure just how the weapon functioned against a human. At any rate he was definitely unconscious. The question was how long would he remain so … and what would happen if they had to use the weapon again …

Gray Wolf came up far enough to help them carry the agent's body back to the ground at the base of the rocks. He concurred that the man was unconscious, but he could not determine how long he would remain in that state.

The question now was what to do with the body. When the agent woke up he would presumably know that he had been attacked as he was about to discover something. He would return as soon as possible with a small army to find out what was so valuable here in the butte. They could simply tie him up and keep him hostage. But his office must know where he was going. If he did not return, someone would come looking for him. They had to by some time if they were going to execute the Plan on schedule.

Enela finally came up with another one of her scathingly brilliant ideas. It would take a little time and everyone would have to help, but, once everything was arranged, Gray Wolf would no longer be required and he could leave without learning of the space ship or the wormhole generator. Yes! It was perfect.

Enela suddenly started barking out orders. "Gray Wolf, please stay here and keep our FBI agent under control. Hit him on the head with a rock, if you have to. Ari-Ula, go back to the Valley and get Arina and Hila. Bring a GPS locator from the supply bunker – a good one. Stop by Gray Wolf's cabin on the way back and get his bottle of whiskey, preferably a full one. I'll meet you all back down here."

"You don't need a GPS device," Gray Wolf said. "I saw this guy using one while I was watching him. He should still have it on him."

A quick search of the agent's body turned up the device – and his weapon – which Enela gave to Gray Wolf for safekeeping. While Ari-Ula raced back to the Valley, Enela went to the parking area and used the GPS device to determine the precise location of the agent's car. Enela had previously played with the one in the supply bunker, so that part was easy. Then she used the device to plan a trip, looking at several possible locations until she found one that suited her purposes. Again, she noted the precise coordinates.

Ari-Ula, Arina and Hila arrived just as Enela finished.

"Okay," Enela asked. "How is our human doing?"

"He's starting to come around," Gray Wolf said. "But he's not back with us, yet."

"Good," Enela said. "You three get our human back into his car, in the driver's seat. Make sure he swallows a goodly amount of that whiskey. Enough to keep him passed out for awhile. I'll join you over there in a few minutes."

Enela scampered back up the rocks and returned to the ship. She used the coordinates she had derived to establish a new wormhole, with just the tiniest hint of an earlier time. She set the wormhole to open in about ten minutes and to stay open for the briefest time possible. She hoped it would be no more than a minute. Then she rushed back to the parking area, doing her best to monitor the elapsed time. She knew this would be close.

Arina and Hila had figured out what Enela was up to. As soon as the agent's body was properly filled with alcohol and propped in the driver's seat they thanked Gray Wolf for all his help and told him that his services would no longer be required. He passed Enela on his way back to his cabin and she retrieved the agent's weapon that he had been carrying.

Ari-Ula had also caught onto the plan, "Where are you going to send him?" she asked when Enela arrived at the car.

"Well, we need some time, and we don't really want to hurt him … " Enela started.

"Where?" Ari-Ula asked somewhat more forcefully.

"My human father once told me about this truck stop near Casa Grande. He said all of the drivers stopped there for the 'services' they offered. It took me awhile to figure out what services he was talking about, but I'm sure he meant prostitutes. Casa Grande is about as far from Tucson as we are, so the odometer will check out. I figure by the time they find him and manage to work out what happened, we'll be long gone. We haven't got much time, so let's get ready!"

Enela got the keys out of the agent's pocket and started the car. Then she put his weapon in his hand and fired two shots into the sand, ensuring that the empty casings landed in the car. The loud noise of the shots made everyone jump. Even the agent seemed to rouse for a moment, before resuming his drunken sleep. She removed the magazine, pushed out several more cartridges, and replaced the magazine and the gun.

At that moment, the wormhole sprang to life in front of the car. Enela reached into the car, shoved the gear lever into drive. She leaped back and slammed the door as the car started to roll slowly forward, into the wormhole. In less than a minute the car had disappeared. The wormhole then collapsed with a slight pop.

"I think that's the last we will see of the FBI," Enela said brushing her hands together in a most human manner.

"None the less," said Ari-Ula, "we shall speed up our departure as much as possible. Arina and Hila, can you and your team be ready to depart in two days – or less?"

Arina and Hila looked at each other. The thought of going back in time had been daunting enough. But to do it tomorrow … "We'll manage," they said in unison, to their own surprise. Then they raced back to the Valley to tell their other team members of the schedule change and to start gathering the materiel they would need to take on the journey.

The time soon came for Arina and Hila to travel back in time to save the Elder population from extinction. They had gathered their equipment and as much of the fungus as they and their team members could carry. They had devised a small cart, constructed from some carefully prepared leftover PVC pipes, to carry their equipment and were gathered out on the desert below the cave.

Enela had entered the computations into the wormhole generator and double-checked all of them three times. She was still nervous. She had never set up such a long wormhole, and it was her friends who were going to travel through it. At last she could postpone no longer. She went to the cave opening and went down to the desert floor to say good-bye. She carried a small package with her.

Enela wished everyone good luck and a smooth journey. She went last to Hila and gave her a loving hug.

"What's this?" Hila asked as Enela handed her the package.

"Just a little something I thought you might need." Enela answered quietly. "Use them carefully. They're fully charged, but once you exhaust the charges, they will be about as useful as a couple of small rocks."

Hila looked in the package to see the two extra weapons from the ship.

"Thank you," she said, hugging Enela again. "I hope we don't have any occasion to use them." She didn't sound too sure of that last statement.

"How long until they depart?" Ari-Ula asked nervously. She did not like being out of the Valley for any period. It made her feel vulnerable.

Almost as she spoke there was a quiet poof as the wormhole opened only a few feet from where they were standing. There was another hasty round of good-byes and best wishes while the team gathered their baggage.

There had been some discussion as to how best handle the 'wagon'. If it went through first and got stuck in the sand on the other end, the ones following might trip over it and be injured.

On the other hand, if it followed the group, it might bump into them or roll over them or get stuck on this side and not make the trip. It was finally decided that the last four Elders through the wormhole would drag the wagon, two on either side of the tang.

Hila and Arina started off through the wormhole. Arina was carrying a rock and a piece of paper on which she would endeavor to return a message after they arrived. Hila was carrying the package containing the weapons. Every ten seconds later two more members of the team would go through the wormhole. At last the four with the wagon approached the entry. As they did, the wagon bogged down in the sand. They almost lost their grip and tumbled forward without it. Several other Elders, including Ari-Ana, rushed up and got behind it. With one great push the wagon came free and rolled rapidly into the wormhole, almost dragging the four team members through with it.

Then the remaining Elders waited – anxiously expecting some message from the other end of the wormhole. Someone suggested that it might be a good idea to stand aside and keep a sharp watch for a flying object. The crowd parted, everyone moving to one side or another. Some held up their hands as though protecting themselves from the flying rock.

Ari-Ula looked over at Enela and asked nervously, "How much longer will the wormhole last?"

Enela had actually been expecting that question. She had picked up a wristwatch from the supply bunker. She looked down at the timer she had started when the wormhole opened.

"Only another four minutes," she answered. She hoped that her calculations had been correct. But she had no experience with a wormhole covering such a distance. "What," she thought to herself, "if her timing was far too short and her friends were still traveling through the wormhole when it collapsed? Could that even happen … ?" She immediately dismissed the thought as far too gruesome to even consider. It had not even been determined yet whether an object could travel backward through a wormhole. Theoretically, it was possible to travel both ways. It just wasn't possible to generate a wormhole into the future. Yet, she watched even more intently for the expected missile.

The seconds were flying by all too rapidly. There were barely thirty seconds left when everyone was startled by an object flying out of the wormhole and landing almost exactly in their midst. For a few seconds no one moved. Then Enela jumped forward and picked up the rock wrapped in paper. It was freezing cold to the touch. She felt a sudden pang – the travelers were not prepared for extremely cold weather. She franticly pulled the paper off the rock and tossed the rock away.

Everyone quickly gathered around Enela to hear the message from the past. She spread out the paper and read:

"Very cold trip! Lasted about two minutes. Nothing we couldn't tolerate. All arrived safely. The area is green, weather is warm. Will be ready for you. Anxiously awaiting your arrival."

When Enela finished reading a cheer went up from the crowd. Enela handed the note to Ari-Ula and went back to the cave to shut down the ship and close it up. Everyone was in great spirits as they made their way back to the Valley.

Everyone, that is, except Ari-Ana. She still had a very grim and determined visage.

Chapter 13

Mary Lends a Hand

When Ari-Ula returned to the Valley she convened an emergency meeting of the Council. First, it would be necessary to tell the Elders who were returning to the Valley of the change in schedule. Once all the Councilors were present this took only a few minutes.

The second task was more complicated. Some way had to be found to transport the arriving Elders from Winton to the Valley. It was agreed that they would most likely be arriving by bus – there was no large airport, and no train depot, nearer than Tucson. They had all been warned not to drive. There was no convenient place to park a large number of cars and they could easily be traced – better that they be sold or at least left scattered about the country.

The discussion of possible options went on for some time. No clear solution became apparent. Enela, who had come back to the Council chamber with Ari-Ula, had been sitting on the side of the chamber listening almost half-heartedly. Her random thoughts suddenly began to coalesce. She stood up and brazenly interrupted the deliberations of the Councilors.

"Ari-Ula," Enela said, "I may have a solution for you to consider."

The Councilors immediately ceased their conversation and looked aghast at the person who had so rudely interrupted them. Ari-Ula had an especially dour expression. She had not noticed

Enela sitting in the chamber. "And just what do you think you can add to our deliberations?" she asked.

"Well," Enela began, "I noticed a large sum of money in the supply bunker. I don't imagine we shall have much use for it where we are going, so why not make use of it here. For the price of a new van or SUV, and a fair fee-per-trip, I think I know someone who will transport our people from Winton to the Valley."

"Do tell," said Ari-Ula, her interest somewhat piqued.

"I have a human friend, Mary Gauss, Enela explained." She already knows that I am not exactly human and hasn't shown any great interest in the fact. She's a high school student in Winton and should have plenty of spare time. I think her school is on vacation for the holidays. She could transport the incoming Elders from Winton, or even Tucson, to a point near the Valley."

"What of her parents?" Ari-Ula asked.

"She has no mother and her father seems to leave her pretty much on her own. I don't think he will be a problem." Enela answered.

"Well," said Ari-Ula, "that sounds like a reasonable approach. Can you get in touch with your friend tonight and see if she will be willing to help?"

"I'll try", Enela said, and turned to go.

"Report back to me as soon as you know," Ari-Ula shouted after her. Then she and the other Councilor went back to their review of the departure plan.

Enela raced to the supply bunker. When she got there she made her way to the back, grabbed one of the cell phones and dialed Mary's number.

When Mary answered, Enela was so taken with the sound of her voice that she almost forgot the purpose of her call. After a few minutes it dawned on her that she was on a mission.

"Mary," Enela finally aid, "I have a proposition for you. How would you like to have a new car, all your own?"

The response on the other end was first a stunned silence, then a good laugh. But, Enela persisted and convinced Mary that she was quite serious.

"That's all well and good," Mary said at last, "but it will never work. I'm too young to own a car. Oh, I don't mind being a taxi driver, the money would came in handy. But I can't just go out and buy a car."

That was a quirk Enela had not considered. "But," she countered, "you can drive one. What if someone 'loaned' you one? Long term, say. One that could be yours when you turn 18. Would your father object?"

"I could handle my father," Mary assured Enela. "How can we pull it off?"

"I'm not sure," Enela admitted. "Someone will come to visit you tomorrow. Can you be home? We'll have to start as soon as possible."

It was agreed. Enela said a quick good-bye and hurried back to the Council chamber to tell Ari-Ula. She and the other Councilors were still conferring when Enela arrived. This time she waited patiently before the dais to be recognized. That didn't take long.

Enela explained that Mary was willing to do the driving, but was not old enough to actually buy a car. Ari-Ula suggested that Mary's father buy the car for Mary – as long as the Elders were providing the money.

"I don't think that would be such a good idea," Enela explained. "Professor Gauss doesn't know about us, and I don't think he would – approve if he did." Then she had another idea. "What about Gray Wolf or Billy Eagle?" she asked. "They both know about us and would have no trouble buying a car!"

"To my knowledge Gray Wolf has never driven a car and probably has never had a drivers license," Ari-Ula said. "Billy Eagle would probably object on some legal grounds – aiding and abetting or some such. But," she thought for a moment, "Red Hawk could do it. I'll get in touch with her immediately. How many Gausses do you suppose live in Winton … ?"

The next morning it was all arranged. Enela would take the money from the supply bunker and give it to Gray Wolf. He in turn would take it to Billy Eagle who would hold it for Red Hawk. She would pick up the money, go get Mary and take her to the car dealer and purchase a suitable vehicle to act as the Elder taxicab. Mary would get the car and a suitable sum to cover her expenses. Whenever Mary transported anyone to the Valley, she would get a sizeable bonus. Red Hawk would put any leftover money to a good purpose.

The councilors, with their combined mental effort, were able to send out a message to all of the Elders. But they could not receive individual replies. All that they knew was that the other Elders would be coming into Winton by bus.

When Mary's father got home and saw the new car in the driveway, he understandably wanted an explanation. Mary was ready for him, though convincing her father was touch-and-go for a while.

"I got a job over the holiday break," she said. "I get to use the car as part of my pay."

"And just what kind of a job pays so well?" the Professor asked.

"I'm running a taxi service. I have to meet every bus that comes into town and pick up certain people."

"What kind of 'certain people'? And where do you take them?"

"I don't know which people. I just hold up a sign and take whoever comes over out to the reservation. Sometimes, I may not get any passengers; sometimes I may have to make more than one trip. But I get paid just to meet each bus."

The next question was tougher, but Mary was ready.

"Just who on the reservation has money enough to pay for all of this?" Her father was more suspicious than curious.

"The manager of the casino in Wakulla", Mary lied. She rightly suspected that her father would never go out to the reservation to verify her story. She also had been told that the casino staff would back up her story.

It wasn't perfect, but, with a little more schmoozing, Mary's father seemed to be satisfied. Mary started her rendezvous with incoming buses.

Meeting the daytime busses was not a problem. But when she realized that she would have to get up at 3:00 AM every weekday to meet the overnight express from Phoenix, she began to rethink her bargain. In the end she learned to take frequent catnaps whenever she had the chance.

Then, there were other benefits. The councilors had posted a continuous watch at the cave dwellings to lead any new arrivals into the Valley. Enela had nothing better to do than monitor the settings in the ship and ensure that enough sunlight was getting into the cave to keep the fuel cells fully charged. That was enough of an excuse to go join the monitor on duty. She was allegedly keeping her company while she waited; but her real reason was to be on hand whenever Mary arrived.

While the monitor led the new arrivals to the Valley, Enela and Mary usually had considerable time together. Sometimes they would sit in the car and talk, sometimes they would lay a blanket out on the sand and enjoy the sun or shade as the mood struck.

Mary would talk about her life in school, in the town, problems with her father, how she missed her mother. Enela usually just listened. She had never experienced school or life in a community. Her human parents had always kept her indoors, lest her odd appearance become too noticeable. But when Mary talked about family problems, Enela could, and did, readily join in the conversation.

When Mary spoke of boys or girls that she knew and liked, Enela always felt a bit of a pang. It was then that she would snuggle closer. There were two humans of whom Mary spoke most often: Ted and Karen. Apparently Mary had engaged in sex with both of them at least once. She told of sneaking each of them into her bedroom. Enela very much wished that Mary would invite her to her bedroom. But it never quite came to that.

One day as they were sitting in Mary's car, Enela got another of her brilliant ideas.

"Teach me to drive," she begged.

Mary looked at Enela with much amusement. "Enela, you aren't tall enough to see out the windshield! And if you sit on something, you could never reach the pedals."

"You could see for me," Enela suggested. "It would only be out here in the desert. What harm could it do?"

Mary continued to protest for a while, but, in the end, she gave in. "Okay, but only for a few minutes. And you have to promise to do just what I tell you, when I tell you."

Enela instantly agreed and the two switched places in the car. In short order, Mary had shown Enela how to start the car, how to steer it and how to use the pedals. Enela shifted into 'drive' and started moving slowly about the parking area. Mary gave her strict instructions to stay off the accelerator until she had mastered all of the other controls.

Enela was ecstatic! She did have problems seeing the ground out of the windshield, but Mary helped by warning of obstacles that she had to avoid. After some twenty minutes, Enela had proven to be a pretty fair driver.

The lesson was far too short, because Mary had to return to Winton to meet another bus. This time there were no Elders on board, so she didn't return to the Valley.

Several days passed in this manner. Sometimes there would not any passengers on a given day and Mary would have no reason to come out to the Valley, but she would come anyway. She and Enela were becoming more and more attached to each other. Finally, Mary's curiosity got the best of her.

'Enela, why am I bringing your people out here to the desert? Are you having some sort of a family reunion?"

Enela didn't answer at once. The question had reminded her most forcibly of the fact that she would soon be leaving and would never see Mary again. She was so enjoying these days that she did not want to face the future. Mary just sat there looking at her expectantly. To her it was a simple question and deserved some answer.

Finally, Enela said softly, "It is something like a family reunion. All of our people have been summoned back here."

"There is more, isn't there," Mary said quietly. She sensed that there was bad news in the offing.

"Yes," Enela almost whispered. "When everyone has returned we will be leaving. All of us."

"Leaving? Where are you going? You will be back – won't you?" Mary really didn't want to hear the answer she knew was coming.

"I can't say where we are going," Enela replied. "But we will not be back – ever."

"You're telling me that we will never see each other again, aren't you," Enela was staring straight ahead. She did not see the tear edging its way out of Mary's eye. "When will you be leaving?" Mary had to ask; it was better to know …

"I can't say exactly," Enela said. "I think we are expecting about thirty or forty to join us. Some twenty have already returned. We should be leaving within the week."

"What happens if I just don't bring any more people out here?" Mary wasn't really suggesting that she would mutiny, but she was willing to engage any hope. Then she asked softly, "I don't suppose that I could go with you …"

"Oh, no!" Enela replied, almost too quickly. "We're taking a big enough risk as it is. There is no way you could join us," Enela sighed. "Besides," she added, "you are going to be a multi-millionaire in a few months. You don't want to miss that, do you."

Mary's eyes were suddenly wide open and dry. "I haven't even looked at that ticket. Do you mean it's a winner!?"

Enela just smiled and said, "Be sure you hang onto that ticket. It should finance your future."

The two just sat in silence and watched the afternoon sun sink toward the horizon. Then it was time for Mary to meet the Tucson bus. She very reluctantly bid Enela good-bye and headed back to Winton.

Enela wandered slowly over to the base of the cliff. She stopped there and leaned against the rock face, watching the sunset. She slowly sank down to the ground and clutched her knees. Her eyes had grown too cloudy to any longer see the sun. She knew she had to make a decision. She sat there for a long time before she finally rose and walked back to the Valley.

Chapter 14

Night of Bliss

The Lodge to which Jonas Gauss belonged had been a long time fixture in Winton. He had joined the Lodge many years ago. When he had arrived in Winton he was lured to it as a haven from the aggravation of having to deal with political correctness and the many illegal aliens and Indians which were overrunning the area.

He noted, thankfully, that were very few blacks in Winton, but there were more than enough Mexicans to make up for any dearth of low-life blacks. The Lodge didn't admit any non-whites to membership. They accepted only men and were pledged not to discriminate on the basis of race or color or national origin. They also thoroughly 'investigated' all applicants. Since one could not become a member except on a unanimous ballot, it was easy for a black ball to be cast against any unsavory applicants. No one ever asked how a brother voted.

Lodge meetings were a dry and boring affair, but the Lodge provided a cool respite for lunch or dinner. There was a bar that served any beverage a member could wish.

A few years after he joined the Lodge, Jonas had been elected Exalted Master. After serving his time as the leader of the Lodge he retired from active participation in Lodge affairs. Jonas frequently dropped in for lunch. He would also come over after his last afternoon class and join in a few hands of cards, and a few drinks, before dinner.

Mary was acting more and more independently, so he did not concern himself about providing dinner for her. It was generally her province to make *him* dinner. But this taxi business kept her so busy that she seldom had the time and he didn't complain.

Some of the brothers, who had seen Mary at the bus depot, even asked Jonas what she was doing. A few expressed some concern that she was catering to a bunch of 'jigapoos'. Jonas usually just brushed them off, saying it was Mary's concern. But what she was doing still bothered him.

The Winton bus depot was at a convenience store located near the center of the town. The store was owned by an Indian named Rajendra Patel. He was generally just called Raj by his customers. Coming from India, he was considered an Aryan and thus 'white', despite his dark skin tone. Even Jonas and his Lodge brothers accepted him as part of the Winton landscape. They often stopped in to fill their gas tanks and pass the time of day with Raj. But they never asked him to join the Lodge.

For the first few days all went well. Mary would be at the bus depot before the bus was scheduled to arrive. Then she would hold up a sign that said, 'ELDER', and wait around to see if she had any clients. She quickly learned to recognize the Elders. They were, of course, far shorter than the average person. And it was impossible for them to completely conceal their white skin.

The first few arrivals came off quite well. There were never more than five or six Elders on a bus and Mary was able to squeeze them all into her car for the trip to the desert. The Tuesday afternoon bus provided the first real problem. There were ten Elders on the bus and there was no way that Mary could fit them all in her vehicle.

"I'm sorry," she told them, "but some of you are going to have to wait here until I get back. I'll hurry as fast as I can." The Elders agreed that six would go with Mary on the first trip and the other four would wait at the convenience store until she returned. Mary loaded the car and took off for the desert.

The remaining Elders browsed among the shelves, doing their best to stay out of sight. At first Raj thought that they might be trying to shoplift. He kept a sharp eye on them, but he could never catch them actually taking anything, so he eventually gave up. He decided that they really were just waiting for their taxi ride. He even offered to call them a local taxi, but they quietly demurred.

About that time Ted Johnson stopped by to fill up his truck. As he went inside to pay for the gas he caught a glimpse of the waiting Elders. Then he walked closer to get a good look. He snorted in disgust as he walked back to the counter.

"What are them jigapoos doing here?" he asked Raj as he handed him the gas money.

"They are just customers," Raj answered.

"Since when are you serving their kind?" Ted snarled. "You know we don't do business in places that cater to them. You do want to keep our business, don't you?"

"Please," Raj pleaded quietly, "They are bus passengers. I have to cater to them or I will lose my contract with the bus company. I can't afford to lose that contract … I have to treat them as any other customers. They will soon be gone."

"What?" Ted was squinting disgustedly in the direction of the Elders. "Are these the people that Mary Gauss is carting around in that fancy new SUV of hers? How come she hasn't picked them up?"

"She has already left with a car full," Ray answered. "I am sure that she will be right back."

"Well, I'm goin' over to the Lodge," Ted said as he scooped up his change. "We'll see what the brothers have to say about a bunch of jigapoos takin' over your store."

"Please wait; they will soon be gone," Raj pleaded to Ted's back.

Ted's statement about going to the Lodge was just bluster at the time. But the more he thought about it, he decided he would drive over to the Lodge. There he chanced upon Jonas Gauss whose last class had ended at 2:00 that afternoon. Jonas was sitting with a couple of the Brothers nursing a beer. Ted joined the group and related his experience at the bus stop. Some of the Brothers commiserated with Ted over the sudden arrival of these odd strangers. Jonas' face subtly reflected his disgust with the situation, but he took a slightly different line.

"At least these people aren't staying around town," he said slowly and deliberately. "Mary has been carting them all out to the Indian reservation as fast as they arrive. Haven't seen any of them come back in town. Guess they know where they aren't wanted."

"Yeah," said one of the Brothers. "But I want to know what they are doing around here. I haven't ever seen their like around here before."

"I think there was a family of them living somewhere out there in the desert," Jonas said. "I've seen one or two of them in town on occasion. But they seem to keep to themselves."

"Well, I still don't like it," Ted said. First, it was the Indians that started coming into town taking things over, getting drunk and generally causing a mess. Then it was the Mexicans. It started with just a few then all of a sudden they're all over the place. You can't walk down the street without bumping into them."

"Since when have you ever 'walked down the street'?" another Brother interrupted.

"Never mind," Ted retorted. "You know what I mean. After the Mexicans, we got those Asians like Raj. Seems like they've bought up all the convenience stores that the Mexicans weren't running. Now it's these new jigapoos. Pretty soon there ain't goin' to be any room left for us white folk."

"Seems to me," Jonas pointed out, "that they are a tad whiter than you are, Ted." Ted took a long slow pull on his beer, giving Jonas a knowing sneer. "But, I agree with you that it would be better if we never saw them again."

"What's Mary doing with these people?" a Brother asked Jonas.

"She says she's taking them out to the Wakulla casino. I have no idea what happens after that. Maybe they're part of a new act at the casino. I make it a point not to go out there unless

190

I am teaching a class at the old butte. Maybe they're just going there to meet their kin."

Ted slugged down the rest of his beer and got up to leave. "I'll see you in a bit," he said. "You staying around for the meeting tonight?" Several heads nodded.

* * * * * * * * * * * * * * * * *

Meanwhile, Enela was on her way to the Council Chamber. Ari-Ula had 'requested' her presence. Enela didn't want to think about why Ari-Ula wanted to see her, but she had already made up her mind that if it involved Mary, there was going to be a fight. All the way to the Council Chamber Enela had been preparing in her mind for just such a confrontation. When she entered, her expectations were suddenly dismissed.

"Thank you for coming so promptly," Ari-Ula said as Enela walked in the doorway. "There has been a change in our schedule. The last of our people will be arriving in Winton today. There is no need to wait any longer. Please arrange for our departure tomorrow afternoon – say about 4:00 PM. Will that be a problem?"

"No, Ari-Ula," Enela stammered. "I can do that."

Ari-Ula noted the tone of Enela's voice. "Is there anything wrong?

"No, no," Enela said quickly. "I just didn't expect us to be going so soon – so permanently … "

"I know," Ari-Ula assured Enela. "Just think of it as a great adventure. And tomorrow we will all be joining our people." Ari-Ula rushed off to attend to other matters.

"Yes," Enela thought, "I will be joining our people, but I will be leaving Mary forever." Elders frequently became friends and formed attachments for each other, but 'love' was a purely human concept. The Elders did not understand it. Enela wondered if she were so different, so altered by her years of living as a human, that she had somehow incorporated the human concept of love.

Enela hurried out to the cave that held the ship to make her final corrections in the settings for the wormhole generator. The self-destruction settings were another problem. They obviously could never be tested. Enela was not sure that they would really work. She wished that Hila was still there to confirm her settings. The more she thought about it, the more she doubted that they would work. She looked at the manual for some guidance – it had always solved all of her other problems. But self-destruction was never even hinted at.

Enela entered the new settings. Then she double-checked them. When she was sure that all was in readiness for departure the next day she closed the ship and went out to the parking area to wait for Mary.

Mary arrived shortly after noon with a carload. The new arrivals quickly doffed their human clothing and Lina led them off to the Valley.

"I've got to go right back for another load," Mary told Enela. "There were too many to fit in the car."

"Let me go with you," Enela pleaded. "I can practice driving on the way. I'll even ride in the rear on the way back!"

"Enela, it's just not safe. What if you were seen?"

"I don't care anymore!" Enela said. "I just want to spend my last hours here with you."

"Last hours!" Mary exclaimed. "Then you are really leaving? Soon?"

"Yes," Enela answered quietly. "We leave tomorrow."

Mary conceded. "You can drive out to the highway. Then you'll have to duck down while I drive into town."

"Enela readily agreed and climbed into the car behind the wheel. Mary got in opposite her and the two took off for town.

Picking up the remaining Elders was uneventful. But Raj seemed quite relieved to see them leave his store.

* * * * * * * * * * * * * * * * *

Ted had conjured up a plan. He just hoped he wasn't too late. He got into his truck and headed back to the bus station. As he waited at a traffic light he saw Mary Gauss pass by heading out to the highway leading north to the reservation. She had the people from the bus in the car with her.

Ted had a problem. He was in the right lane, but wanted to turn left to follow Mary. He solved the problem by gunning the engine the instant the light turned green and pulling around the car on his left. There was some horn honking, but no blue lights. So far, so good.

193

As Mary passed through the intersection at Division St on the way back to the desert she heard a sudden squeal of tires and a honking of horns behind them. She looked back in her rearview mirror, but couldn't see anything. Just another Friday afternoon driver she assumed.

Ted stayed well back from Mary. Just keeping her in sight up ahead. He knew she was going to the reservation, he just wasn't too sure what she was going to do when she got there.

Traffic on the highway consisted of several cars headed north. They seemed to like the shortcut through the reservation. Mary quickly turned off on the path leading to the ruins. She knew that Enela wanted to drive over the desert, but Enela was in the back and Mary didn't feel like stopping and rearranging everyone, so she just kept on driving.

As they approached the turn-off to Wakulla, Ted was behind a string of cars, peeking out around the right side to catch Mary's car when she turned to go to the hotel. But the turn-off came and went and there was no sign of Mary turning towards Wakulla. Ted looked around in a panic. Where was she? Was she still up ahead or had he missed her somehow?

Then Ted noticed a small plume of dust off in the desert behind him to his left. While he was watching the Wakulla turn, she had turned off into the desert toward the mountains. So much for the story about the Wakulla casino. Ted turned around as quickly as he could and headed back. The road to the pueblo butte was barely a path through the sand. Ted shifted his truck into 4-wheel drive and turned off the pavement

Ted followed the path carefully - and slowly. He did not want to raise a dust plume to advertise his presence. Mary wasn't as careful. It was relatively easy to follow the plume she was raising. After a while Ted realized that Mary's dust plume had disappeared. She had stopped somewhere ahead of him.

Mary had arrived at the parking lot and unloaded. Lina was again there to conduct the newcomers back to the Valley. Mary and Enela collected the clothing and saw the others off. After Mary stored the clothes in the car, she pulled out an old blanket and carried it up to the front to the car, which provided a little shade from the afternoon sun.

Ted wasn't familiar with this area and had no idea what if anything was up ahead. He could see two large buttes and the mountains beyond them. Ted stopped the truck behind a large mesquite bush, grabbed a pair of binoculars from behind the seat and got out.

Nothing was readily visible from the ground, so Ted climbed into the bed of the truck and then up onto top of the cab. From this elevated position he could see Mary's car stopped in a clearing next to the closer butte. Then he recognized the butte. It was where the cliff dwellings were located – the ones that Jonas used in his classes.

Ted moved the binoculars back to the car. He expected Mary to be moving back to the highway, but she wasn't. She had taken a blanket out of her car and had carried it to the front of her car. She appeared to be talking to someone. She shook out the blanket and placed it on the ground in front of the car. Then she apparently sat down on the blanket. She was   out of sight.

195

"So this was the last trip?" Mary asked as she started to spread the blanket.

"Yes," Enela answered quietly. "That's what Ari-Ula told me this morning. We will be leaving tomorrow."

"You never have said where you are going," Mary sat down on the blanket.

"I can't, Mary," Enela was almost in tears. "But once we do leave we will never – ever – see each other again."

"It sounds so final," Mary sighed. "You aren't going to commit suicide or anything?" It was a sudden and very unpleasant thought.

"Oh, no," Enela answered. "We will still be alive – I hope. It's just that we will be so very far away."

"There is no place so far away on this planet that we can't get together again as soon as I get my lottery winnings," Mary was quite positive about that.

"That's right," Enela agreed, "… on this planet … "

Mary began to see the light, but before she could say anything, Enela had another thought.

"When I was living with the humans," she said, "if two people liked each other a lot they often spent the night together at one of their homes. It was called a 'sleep-over'. Can I spend the night at your house?"

"Oh, Enela," Mary was in anguish. "My father is home. If he ever saw you he would kill us both."

"But if we were in your room, he wouldn't see us."

"In my room … " Mary was thinking wildly. "This is his lodge night, he won't be home until late. And he has a breakfast at the lodge tomorrow morning. He will probably leave early for that and be gone for hours. Maybe it would work … But we would have to be very careful … "

"Let's do it!" Enela was excited about the possibility.

"All right, but I will have to drive," Mary said. Almost before she had finished speaking Enela had started for the passenger door. Mary folded the blanket and stowed it in the back and they started back toward town.

Several thoughts passed through Ted's mind as he watched Mary's car. There had been times in his past when he had taken a blanket out of his car and spread it on the ground. In almost all cases his goal in doing so was to coax some girl into having sex with him. Ted watched more intently – surely this couldn't be the situation here. Was Mary Gauss having sex with these creatures? Impossible!

Ted climbed down, jumped in his truck and headed back to the highway. He did not want Mary to see him out here on the desert. Ted did his best to leave as small a dust plume as possible and still get back to the highway before Mary could see him.

Enela saw it before Mary did. "Look up there, is that someone else driving toward the highway?"

Mary squinted hard and saw the small dust plume ahead of them on the road. She couldn't imagine who would have been out on the path to the ruins. It was probably just a tourist who made a wrong turn, but still, there was no reason to be reckless – she slowed down to give the other driver plenty of time to reach the highway ahead of her.

Once he reached the highway Ted turned toward the Wakulla turn-off, went past it and turned around to face Winton. He wanted to be able to follow Mary no matter which way she went. He parked at the side of the road just in time to see Mary pull out on the highway and head back to town.

Ted followed Mary. More closely this time. He did not want to lose her in town traffic. As they drove toward town he strained to look into her vehicle. He could not see whether she had a passenger.

As far as Mary was concerned the rest of the drive to her house was uneventful. They stopped at the Goodwill store so Mary could drop off the Elders' clothing. Enela just crouched own in the seat while they were there and in a matter of minutes they were off again.

Mary pulled into her driveway and parked in front of the garage door. She got out of the car and looked around carefully. She wanted to make sure that there was no one out working in the yard who might see them. The area seemed to be clear so she motioned Enela to get out on her side of the car. Enela was grinning in anticipation as she climbed over. Mary put her arm around her and quickly led her into the house.

Ted watched Mary stop at the Goodwill store and give them the clothing that her original passengers had been wearing. Then he followed her as she drove on straight to her house and pulled into the driveway. Ted waited about a block away and watched through the binoculars. He could see Mary get out of the car and look around. Then Ted watched as Enela also got out of the car and the two of them went into the house.

Ted couldn't believe what he had just seen. He didn't want to believe that Brother Jonas' daughter was somehow involved with these new interlopers. But he had to believe his own eyes. Then another thought hit him – was Jonas involved? Was Jonas just reporting what his daughter had told him or was he actively supporting her involvement with these things? Ted started the truck and drove back to the Lodge. It was going to be an interesting meeting tonight.

Chapter 15

Departure

Mary's house was a one-story ranch style. It looked very much like all the other houses in the neighborhood. The lawn was sunken to hold water when it rained. The was a small pool out in back, but the yard only had a chain link fence around it; so Mary and Enela could not go swimming without the risk of being spotted by neighbors.

The inside of the house was not remarkable. The usual living room and dining room. One of the three bedrooms had been converted to an office by Mary's father. It had a small desk, a large worktable and was full of books and relics. Enela thought it was fascinating, but Mary cautioned against moving anything out of place and the two left the room.

Mary's room was in the front corner of the house. It was done entirely in pink with white furniture. There was a double bed with a canopy, a desk, a chest and an old toy box at the foot of the bed. There was also a set of bookshelves loaded to overflowing with books and curios. The top of the chest contained a wide assortment of cosmetics and perfumes and there were more on the desk. Clothes were scattered on the bed and floor.

"I hope you like it," Mary said. "I can wander around the house, but you're going to be stuck in here for quite a while."

"I think it's beautiful," Enela said. "What sort of creature is that?" she added, pointing to a picture on the wall.

"It's a unicorn." Mary answered. "My father gave me the picture and made the frame for it. Unicorns are mythological animals; they never really existed."

"Hmm, I wouldn't be too sure about that," Enela mused. "What do you use all these for?" she asked, scrutinizing all the bottles and tubes on the chest and desk.

"I use them to make myself beautiful and to smell good."

"I bet you would look just as beautiful and smell just as good to me without them," Enela offered. "Why don't we see?" she asked impishly. "Let's take a shower!"

The idea surprised Mary and then enchanted her. She quickly removed her clothes and she and Enela headed to the bathroom. The water was warm and the two took the opportunity to examine each others body closely and carefully. Enela marveled at the complexity of Mary's vulva and Mary was intrigued by Enela's tiny but functional breasts and single excretory opening. They took their time washing and only gave up the cascading water when it began to turn cold.

After they had dried and Mary had combed out her hair they raided the kitchen for food for Mary and water for both of them. Enela picked up a large sauce pan to use as a chamber pot should urge arise and the bathroom be off limits. Then they retired to Mary's room. Mary assured Enela that her father would knock before entering, giving Enela plenty of time to hide before he came in.

Mary spent some time drying and styling her red hair. Enela was used to humans having hair, but she did not remember either of her human parents ever being so fastidious with it. Once her hair was dry Mary selected some of her cosmetics and prepared to 'do her face'. At that point Enela objected. She thought that Mary looked just fine without any additional coloration. In fact she insisted on it. Mary finally gave up trying and complied with Enela's wishes.

At first the two just sat on Mary's bed and talked. They covered many topics, both great and small. But neither of them touched on the one topic that brought them together for this one night.

Suddenly, Mary noticed the lateness of the hour. She jumped up and turned on the small TV that sat on her toy chest. She set the volume low, so that they could continue talking.

"That will cover the sound of our voices," she explained. "My father will be home anytime now. He usually looks in on me before he goes to bed. But he knocks before he comes in."

Almost as Mary spoke they heard the sound of a car pulling into the driveway. A few moments later the front door opened and they could hear steps in the hall. Jonas Gauss went to his office, to his bedroom and then back out to the kitchen before he finally returned to knock on Mary's door. Mary quickly slipped into a robe and motioned Enela to hide in her closet.

"Come in, Dad." Mary responded to the knock.

Her father opened the door and peered into the room. "Everything OK?" he asked.

"Just fine, Dad" Mary answered. "How was Lodge?"

"The usual," he answered. "I have to be up early in the morning to help with the breakfast at the Lodge. I'm going to hit the hay. Good night." He closed the door and moved across the hall to his own room.

Mary got up and let Enela out of the closet. The two just stood there, as if savoring the moment. Then Enela gently reached up and kissed Mary. Her kiss was both tentative and passionate. It lasted for but a second, but it was quickly followed by a second and then a third. Then all pretense was cast aside and the two embraced in total passion.

Mary doffed her robe and led the way back to the bed and lay down, pulling Enela next to her. Enela's hands quickly started caressing those places she had investigated during their shower. She touched lightly at first then with more firmness and lust. Mary returned the favor. She remembered what Enela had said when they were at the ruins. Her hands began stroking Enela's legs and thighs.

The two lay on the bed each passionately kissing and caressing the other. Mary's crotch was dripping wet and quivering to Enela's every touch.

"Please," Mary panted, tell me how I can get you as excited as I am!"

"Stroke the inside of my thighs," Enela panted as she rolled over onto her back and spread her legs. Mary moved on top of Enela and did as she was bidden, first with her hands, then with her legs. After only a minute or so Mary felt something reaching up between her legs, probing as though it were searching for an opening. Mary reached down and felt a thin cool penis extending from between Enela's legs. Almost instinctively she guided it up into her vagina.

The penis slipped easily inside. It began to pulse slowly. Enela shifted her position slightly and the penis penetrated even further. There was no frantic thrusting, no urgency at all. Enela pressed her body against Mary's clit. There was a gentle rhythmic movement. Mary could feel her passion building, growing greater with every movement until she could no longer stand it. She grabbed Enela franticly kissing her deeply and tightly to avoid crying out with the sudden release of tension. Mary didn't feel the penis retracting. At first she was afraid that her throes of passion had spoiled the moment for Enela. But the latter just lay there quietly exhausted as though she had no intention of ever moving again. The two bodies remained entwined together for some time.

When Mary got up some time later to turn off the TV set she thought she felt some liquid running down her leg. The room was dark so she couldn't get a good look and she had no desire to spoil evening by turning on a light and hunting up a tampon, so she just said to hell with it and went back to bed. She would deal with the mess tomorrow.

Mary and Enela did not get much sleep that night. Every time either of them woke up she would begin stroking and caressing the other. No overture was ever rejected. But Enela's penis did not make another appearance. She assured Mary that this was perfectly normal and did not mean that she was not thoroughly enjoying her ministrations. For her part, Mary simply lost count of the orgasms that Enela managed to induce.

Neither of them heard Jonas Gauss get up and leave the house at seven.

Ted had seen Jonas at the Lodge meeting the previous evening, but had decided against telling him then about Mary's activities. Lodge meetings were supposed to be harmonious, and Ted did not think that Jonas would take the news very well. Yet, he knew he had to tell him eventually, so he showed up at the Lodge breakfast.

"Jonas, can I speak to you for a minute?" Ted asked as he stuck his head into the kitchen where Jonas was tending the grill.

"Sure, Ted," Jonas answered. He called for one of the other Brothers to take over his spot at the grill and followed Ted to an empty corner of the dining room.

"What's up?" Jonas asked when they were suitably alone.

"Well," Ted began, "You know how you said that Mary was taking those jigapoos to the Wakulla casino … "

"Don't call them 'jigapoos', Ted," Jonas interrupted. "They aren't black; they are whiter than we are."

"Well, whatever you want to call them," Ted continued. His exasperation giving him the impetus to continue. "They aren't going to the Wakulla casino, or anywhere else in Wakulla.

Mary took this last batch to the ruins where you have your classes."

"To the cliff dwellings?" Jonas was truly confused. "How do you know that?"

"Yesterday," Ted said, "when I left here, I met up with Mary on her way out of town with that group she left at the bus stop – and followed her. Before she got to the Wakulla turn-off, she turned left and headed straight to the ruins."

Jonas made no comment; he just stared straight ahead, so Ted continued, "When they got out of the car, them weirdoes took off all of their clothes and headed somewhere around the butte."

"How do you know all this?" Jonas wasn't quite ready to buy all of this new information at face value. "If you could see Mary, she could see you. What if this was just an act?"

"I made sure she didn't see me," Ted answered. "I stayed well back so she couldn't see the truck. I drove real slow across the sand so I wouldn't raise a dust plume. When she stopped at the ruins I pulled in behind a mesquite tree. The I took my binoculars and climbed up on the cab of the truck. I had a pretty good view, but she wouldn't notice a thing."

"All right," Jonas said. "So she didn't take them to the casino. That doesn't really mean anything."

"Except that she lied to you about what she was doing," Ted felt a certain advantage and was determined to finish his story and then duck for cover. "And there's more. After the others took off for wherever, Mary stayed behind, took out a blanket laid it out in front of her car and sat down on it. She had to

206

be talking to one of them."

"Did you actually see her talking to one of them?" Jonas asked.

"No, not really," Ted admitted. "But there was no one else around, and why would she just sit on a blanket out there by herself?"

"What happened then?" Jonas persisted.

"As soon as she picked up the blanket and headed to her car," Ted continued his story, "I got back in the truck and took off for the highway; I didn't want her to catch me there. She headed back to Winton,"

"Back to Winton?" Jonas was confused. "Did you follow her? Where did she go in Winton?"

"Yeah, I followed them, just far enough back so that I wasn't too obvious. She made a stop at the Goodwill store where she dumped off all of the clothing those weirdoes were wearing. Then she went to your house. I saw Mary get out and take one of those whatevers into the house with her."

"What!" Everyone in the room looked at Ted and Jonas, wondering what had brought out so sudden an exclamation. Jonas didn't know whether to consider the whole thing some crude joke, or …

"I swear, Jonas," Ted said, "as a Brother I wouldn't lie to you. I'm just telling you what I saw."

"So she took one of them into the house," Jonas was trying to find an acceptable explanation. "They probably left after a few minutes."

"Actually," Ted said, "I waited around for over an hour before I came over here for the meeting. They didn't show any signs of leaving. As a matter of fact, as it was getting dark, the only light I saw was coming from Mary's bedroom."

Jonas was no longer standing there quietly by Ted. He was moving very quickly toward the door, shouting out to those in the kitchen that he had to leave and would be back soon. Jonas ran out to his car and was soon driving rapidly toward his house.

Mary and Enela had just managed to get out of bed. Mary was thinking of another shower and some breakfast. Enela was trying not to think that she would soon be leaving Mary forever. They both froze in place when they heard a car pull into the driveway and come to a tire-squealing stop.

"That sounds like my father's car!" Mary shrieked as a car door slammed. "Oh, my God, he shouldn't be here!"

"I'll hide in the closet again," Enela suggested.

"No! I don't like this," Mary insisted. "If he finds you here he's likely to kill both of us! You've got to get out of the house."

Before either of then could even get out of the bedroom, the front door slammed open. Mary spun around and threw open a window. It was the only chance left.

"Get out the window," Mary shouted in a whisper. "Here, take my car and drive back to the reservation. I'll stall my father as long as I can and pick the car up at the ruins later." She thrust the keys into Enela's hand as she shoved her out the window and   slammed it shut.

Jonas Gauss burst into Mary's room without taking time to knock. "Where is it?" he demanded.

"Don't you usually knock before coming into my room?" Mary asked indignantly. "I was just going to take a shower – I haven't even got any clothes on."

"Where is it?" her father again demanded.

"Where's what?" Mary asked.

"Don't give me that," her father spat out and pushed Mary roughly back onto the bed. "Ted saw you bringing one of those creatures into our house, yesterday. Where is it?"

Mary saw the figment of an out. "Ted must have been pulling your leg, father," she tried. "I'm being paid to take them out to Wakulla, not to bring them home or take them on any tours."

Jonas walked over to the bed and slapped Mary hard across the face. "Don't lie to me you little bitch!" he shouted. Ted followed you yesterday and told me about you taking them out to the ruins. You didn't go anywhere near Wakulla."

Mary licked a drop of blood from the cut on her lip. She knew her father was a latent white supremacist and a bigot, but this was a side of him that she had not seen before. She was beginning to be afraid – very afraid.

"Enela just stopped in for a visit," Mary offered. "She left after an hour or so." It seemed like a good story. Mary was listening closely so she could to hear her car start. But she heard nothing.

"My, God!" her father recoiled. "Don't tell me you're on a first name basis with one of those things!" He was furious. He felt that he had to relieve his frustrations – and Mary was the only available object. As he stepped toward the bed where Mary lay naked and vulnerable he noticed the disheveled state of the bed. The way the covers had been thrown back on both sides of the bed. The way the pillows both reflected head dents. Even his anger did not dull his mind to the point that the evidence was not obvious.

Jonas reached out and grabbed Mary by the hair and was about to lift her off the bed when a car was started in the driveway.

Once Enela had recovered from her tumble out the window, she got up and peeked back into Mary'' bedroom. She saw Mary's father enter. Enela knew that Elders had the ability to affect humans' minds, but she had never had any training in such activity. Nonetheless, Enela tried to reach into the mind of Jonas Gauss. She tried very hard. What she found was a blackness and hatred that almost overwhelmed her. Try as she might she could not penetrate it or gain any control over it.

Enela tried to reach Mary – to encourage her to fight back and escape. She thought that perhaps she had succeeded a little, but then Mary's father had thrown her onto the bed and the loud argument emanating from the bedroom had attracted attention in the house next door. People were beginning to look out their windows. Enela had no choice left but to flee.

She ran around the corner of the house toward the driveway. Then stopped in her tracks. Jonas Gauss had parked his car directly behind

Mary's. There was no room to move Mary's car forward or backward. Enela almost threw the keys down in disgust, but then she noticed the other keys on the ring. There was another key on the ring very much like Mary's car key. Could it be possible!

Enela ran to Jonas' car and tried the key in the door lock. It turned! Jonas' car was much larger than Mary's – and Enela had no time to make multiple adjustments. She would have to make do just as it was. She climbed in, fitted the key in the ignition and started the car.

Jonas stood at least six feet tall; Enela was barely five feet – when she stretched. Managing to see out the windshield, press the pedals on the floor and steer the thing was not going to be an easy task. Enela backed the car down the driveway. She was actually considering stopping it there and switching to Mary's car. Then she saw Jonas Gauss at the door of the house. There was no stopping now. Enela put the car in drive and headed off down the street at a rather high rate of speed.

Enela searched her mind for the path that Mary had taken on the drive out to the butte. Then she did her best to follow it.

While Mary had taught Enela the basics of driving a car, she had never taught Enela anything at all about speed limit signs, stop signs or traffic lights. After a few near misses – some involving squealing brakes and shouted epithets - Enela learned to drive with the flow of traffic. After that she had fewer problems and soon reached the highway leading to the reservation.

Jonas Gauss had rushed outside the house to see his car moving off down the block, seemingly under its own power and very much without a driver. He just stood there for a minute, stunned and speechless. Then he grabbed his cell phone and dialed the Lodge. To his great relief, Ted answered.

"Ted," he spluttered, "this is Jonas. That jigapoo just stole my car! Get together some of the brothers who have their guns with them and come over to pick me up. We're going out to the desert for target practice."

Jonas didn't wait for Ted to respond. He broke the connection and turned to go back into the house. He had a little business to attend to before the Brothers arrived. When he got to Mary's bedroom, he found it even more cluttered than it had been. A drawer had been pulled out of the chest. The window was wide open. And Mary was gone.

Well, he thought, I will attend to her when she comes home. He went into his bedroom and selected his favorite carbine and some ammunition from the gun rack. Then he went back to the street to wait for his Lodge Brothers. If anyone asked, he would simply tell them he was going on a little hunting trip.

* * * * * * * * * * * * * * * * * * *

Billy Eagle was preparing for another active day in Wakulla. It was the height of the tourist season, and the sleepy little town had taken on a new image as the sightseers poured in to watch the western show. But Billy was not prepared for the visitor who wandered into his office at mid morning.

"Sheriff, I'm Roger Harris, Tucson FBI office." The speaker was a middle-aged man, still quite trim and physically fit. He appeared somewhat incongruous in a business suit. He displayed his ID, put it away and stuck out his hand.

Billy put on his best stoic persona and tried not to show the state of his nerves at the moment. "What can I do for you Mr. Harris?" he asked accepting the extended hand and offering his visitor a seat by his desk.

"One of our agents was sent out here recently to investigate a large excavation in one of the buttes west of here," Agent Harris explained. "Seems the Homeland Security folks have an interest in strange new caves. At any rate our agent ended up in Casa Grande. We don't know why – neither does he. He claimed that he came out here and spoke to you … "

The pause was an obvious invitation for Billy to say something. Billy surveyed his options and said nothing.

"Yeah, well," Harris continued, "I was sent out to finish the job. Are you familiar with the excavation I'm talking about?"

"I'm not sure," Billy offered. "Do you have a map or something?"

Harris reached into his pocket and pulled out a folded piece of paper. When he spread it out on the desk Billy could see that it was a satellite picture of the western end of the reservation. The butte with the cave was small but quite obvious.

"Yes, I recognize the area," Billy said. "I could guide you out there if you like. There aren't any roads into that area and the sand is quite

213

unforgiving – even to four-wheeled vehicles - if you get off the rocky ground." Then he had a second thought… "I am supposed to be part of the show this afternoon," Billy said as he patted the old six-shooter on his hip. "Perhaps we could go out there on Monday."

Agent Harris frowned. "I think I would rather see the place today. It shouldn't take too long. I just need a quick look to make sure some nasty aliens aren't using it to store weapons or the like. I'm sure we'll be back in plenty of time for you to be in the show. I'd even like to see it."

There was no doubt about Agent Harris' intent. He could cause Billy considerable trouble and might even discover the Elders if left to his own devices. "All right," Billy said. "Just let me tell my deputy where I'll be and we can take off. We can use my Jeep."

Billy stepped into the back room and fired up the radio. He called to Gray Wolf, but there was no answer. Billy was getting just a bit nervous. He couldn't stall the FBI agent any longer. If he couldn't get word to Gray Wolf, the Elders would be completely unprepared for their arrival. Billy was worried that someone might really get hurt this time. Billy grabbed a spare handset; maybe there would still be a chance before they got to the butte. Before he went back into the office, Billy also grabbed the carbine that was hanging on the wall.

* * * * * * * * * * * * * * * * * * *

At first Enela thought about stopping at the parking area at the ruins. But the closer she came she decided that would be too obvious. When she got to the butte she veered around it and headed

214

for the canyon where Gray Wolf had his cabin and which led to the passage into the Valley. As Enela neared the canyon she could see several people standing near Gray Wolf's cabin. Now the problem became the practical one of stopping the car without hitting anything – or anyone.

There was a lot of sand and dust kicked up by the tires, but Enela managed to stand on the brake and steer it into a three point landing right next to the corral. When the dust settled, everyone crowded around the car to see who had arrived in so stellar a manner. When Enela staggered out of the vehicle the surrounding faces reflected every emotion from outright disgust to total hilarity.

Everyone was busy brushing off the scattered sand, but Ari-Ula was the first to find her voice. "Enela, what are you doing in that car? Where have you been? What is going on here?"

"I'm sorry, Ari-Ula," Enela began, "but think there may be some trouble. We either need to leave right now or get everyone back in the Valley and give up any thought of leaving for a while."

"What are you talking about?" Ari-Ula was not in a good mood. "The plans have been made and we will follow them. We leave this afternoon. That will give you plenty of time to explain yourself."

Red Hawk, who had been chuckling mightily at Enela's impromptu appearance, sensed the urgency in Enela's voice and demeanor. Whatever was going on appeared to be serious and worthy of note. She gently touched Ari-Ula's shoulder. "Ari-Ula, perhaps we had better listen to Enela's story at once. There may be a proper reason for her request."

"I concur," Ari-Ana spoke out, "if my opinion matters. I feel we may be in peril if we ignore what Enela has to say. We can deal with any possible indiscretions later and elsewhere."

Under such pressure, Ari-Ula had no choice but to relent. "All right, Enela, tell us what happened and why we need to leave so urgently."

"Well, … " Enela started speaking so rapidly that she barely had a chance to take a breath. She feared that if she stopped before she got the whole story out she would never have a chance to finish it. She finally wrapped it up, "…so, since I couldn't take Mary's car, I took Mr. Gauss's car instead. He was so mad at Mary for just being my friend I'm sure he will find a way to come out here after his car. If he does come out here, he will probably want to hurt us, too."

Ari-Ula, Ari-Ana and Red Hawk just looked at each other. Gray Wolf left the group without comment and headed back to his cabin. Red Hawk finally asked the question they had each been pondering, "Enela, how soon can you open a wormhole?"

"Give me ten minutes," Enela answered eagerly. "But I won't be able to hold it open long. Everyone is going to have to move through more quickly than the first group did. About one-second intervals, without stopping."

"Why so fast?" asked Red Hawk.

"The ship gets its power from the sun," Enela explained, "and today is overcast. It takes a lot of power to hold a wormhole open and I have to keep one of the power units in reserve." Enela did

216

not add what she was thinking, "to destroy the ship after we're gone." "Plus," she added aloud, "there are a lot more people to go through this time."

Ari-Ula had another thought … "Enela, can you turn the wormhole around so that the opening faces towards the Valley?"

"Yes, I think so," Enela said curiously.

"Good." said Ari-Ula. "Do so. That will enable the bulk of our people to remain close to the Valley if they should need to retreat. Signal from the cave when you are ready to open the wormhole. Ari-Sona, see that everyone gets out of the Valley and prepare to seal the entrance. But won't actually do so until we are sure that everyone will make it through the wormhole."

Enela sprinted off to the cave to set up the wormhole. Ari-Ula started gathering those who were outside the Valley and Ari-Sona returned to the Valley one last time to chase out any stragglers.

"I'll go see if Enela needs any help," Ari-Ana said, as she moved quickly toward the cave with the ship.

Gray Wolf returned from his cabin to where Red Hawk remained standing. He looked especially worried.

"I just talked to Billy Eagle on the radio," he said. "He is headed our way with another FBI agent. I asked him to take his time, and to keep an eye out for any interlopers from town."

"Now you've got me worried," Red Hawk admitted. "It isn't so bad that the FBI agent sees the Elders if they all get away. But he could be troublesome if he decides he wants to keep a couple of samples around for research purposes. And he could make real trouble for Gray Wolf, Billy and me. Maybe I can help … "

Red Hawk immediately went into a deep trance. She had been practicing this for months now and was getting good at it. Now she would have to do without the aid of the mescal that she usually used. It wouldn't do for the FBI to catch her with traces of illegal drugs in her system.

Red Hawk sent out a call for Taka, her spirit guide. The great hawk was resting in a shady crevice near the top of the Valley butte. Shortly he answered her call, "Greetings, Companion."

"Greetings, Taka," Red Hawk answered. "I have a favor to ask."

"And how do you intend to pay for your favor?" Taka always wanted to keep the balance sheets even. And he did so enjoy the occasional mouse or rabbit, which Red Hawk could point out to him.

"This is an emergency, Taka," Red Hawk countered. "I need your bright eyes and sharp talons. It might even be a tad bit dangerous, so if you are afraid … "

"Taka is not afraid of anything," was the sharp rebuke. "What is it you wish?"

"There are two humans in a vehicle coming from the Indian town," Red Hawk said. "Keep me posted on their travel. You can harass them, but do not attack. They may be more humans in vehicles coming from the big town. Tell me what you see. These you may attack at will; but be careful because they probably will have weapons."

"Taka will do as you ask. It will be fun," was the terse reply.

Enela had made it to the cave and was making the latest corrections to the coordinates. She was working quickly and felt the pressure of being ready in so short a time. She had to recalibrate the arrival place and time due to the earlier departure. If she added a factor of 4096 to the original coordinates, that would do it. No, she had to *subtract* the factor, not add it. It was the original coordinates wasn't it? Or had she changed the values. She wasn't sure, but she had no time to verify the settings. They had to be correct. Then she had to reverse the opening of the wormhole and set the timing. Two hundred people, two at a time at two-second intervals – no make that three-second intervals - would be about five minutes. How long would it take the last power unit to overload the wormhole generator? Certainly more than two minutes, but how much more … ? Well, she wouldn't be here to find out, would she.

Just as Enela had finished her calculations and was making the final settings, Ari-Ana entered the control room.

"The Elders are ready. How are you coming?" she asked.

"I'm through here," Enela answered. "I just have to climb into the equipment closet and set the timer and connect the power unit to destroy the ship. It won't take more than a few seconds." Enela gave the settings on last look and headed out into the corridor.

When the power unit was ready, Enela went back into the control room and hit the switch to activate the wormhole. Ari-Ana took hold of Enela and almost pushed her out of the ship and back into the cave. They went to the cave opening and waved to Ari-Ula. Ari-Ula had been waiting for the signal and immediately waved back. Enela closed the entry to the ship. Everything would work – or not work – automatically from now on. She turned to start the climb down to the desert when something in the distance caught her eye. There was a large plume of dust back toward Winton.

The shimmering entry hole sprang to life below the cave. Ari-Ula began ushering the Elders into the wormhole. They had all been briefed the night before on how to make the trip. All were eager to go. They lined up quietly and somewhat anxiously and, two by two, stepped off into the unknown.

There was a bright flash near the opening of the wormhole. Enela's heart skipped a beat. She didn't know what had caused it and feared there was a problem. She looked carefully, but the flash did not recur and the Elders entering the wormhole did not seem to have noticed anything.

After a couple of minutes it seemed that all was going well. Then there was a muffled explosion back in the canyon as Ari-Sona detonated the explosives that would block any retreat back into the Valley.

Enela watched the progress from the cave. The plume of dust was getting closer, much closer. The vehicles were moving quickly. There was now a second plume, smaller coming from the general direction of Wakulla. It looked as though that plume would intersect the other at the ruins – before everyone had made it through the wormhole. Enela and Ari-Ana quickly climbed down from the cave and joined the others in front of the wormhole.

Ted and Jonas had expected to find Gauss's SUV in the parking area by the ruins, but it wasn't there.

"What now, Jonas?" Ted asked as they came into sight of the parking area.

Jonas did not want to drive across his classroom area, so he suggested that they drive around the right side of the butte. "But stay near the butte or we'll bog down in the sand," he said.

When the rounded the butte they were able to see the Elders ahead of them. "Time for some target practice," Ted exclaimed as he gunned the truck forward. Jonas Gauss leaned out the window with his carbine, but was bouncing too badly to take aim.

Taka had reported his sightings back to Red Hawk. Now it was time for the hawk to have some fun. He dove down on one of the men standing in the back of a pick-up, grabbing him on the shoulder with his sharp talons. Taka immediately let go as the man let out with a yowl, then circled up to strike a man in another truck.

The screams from the hawk's attack startled everyone. Some of the men turned to fire at Taka, but the moving trucks made hitting the fast flying hawk impossible. One man was leaning out a window with a pistol. Taka took aim and hit his arm hard and fast. Howling in pain, the man dropped his gun and quickly pulled back inside the vehicle, cranking up the window.

Taka had done well. He had delayed the men's ability to take any action against the Elders.

But he had not prevented it. Ted stopped his truck directly below the cave, so that the Brothers would have a steady platform from which to shoot. The other trucks lined up beside and behind him. Those with rifles used the truck cab as a shooting stand. The Elders were not even aware of their presence until the first one suddenly fell wounded.

Those closest to the wormhole continued into it at a fast run. Some of the others scattered and tried to find shelter among the few cacti and mesquite trees. Ari-Ana, who was brining up the end of the line, ducked down by a small mesquite tree as additional shots rang out.

Red Hawk called out to Taka. One more attack on the lead truck.

Taka heard and obeyed. She dove down on one of the men in the back of the truck, then skipped forward to Jonas and Ted. They all screamed in pain.

But Taka had taken too long in the attack. One of the men in the rear truck had seen the hawk diving down and drew a bead on the bird as it soared off skyward. The shot sounded and feathers flew from Taka. The great hawk tipped sideways and sailed downward to the ground at the corner of the butte.

"Let's go!" Enela shouted as she ran to the wormhole. "Come on! Move it!" she exhorted the others. "Run!" Ari-Ana joined in, grabbing a couple of the Elders closest to her and pushing them to the wormhole. Enela stopped to gather up the Elder who had been wounded by the first shot. All of them were running as fast as they could toward the shimmering wormhole. Enela guessed that only seconds remained.

Billy Eagle and Agent Harris were still bouncing along the sand toward the butte. When Billy saw the trucks arrive he decided that it was more important for him to get over there than to worry about what Harris might see. He took a direct path across the sand and pushed the little Jeep as fast as it would go. Billy had the steering wheel and gearshift to hang onto, Agent Harris was bouncing so much he couldn't get his hand onto anything stable. As soon as Billy judged that he was within range of his carbine he unhooked Harris' seatbelt, twisted the wheel hard to the left and told him to "Jump!"

The Jeep locked into the loose sand and flipped over onto its side. Billy and Harris landed on the sand behind the Jeep, which was in a perfect position to provide cover from any gunfire that might be directed their way. Without hesitation, Billy propped his carbine up on the Jeep and took aim on one of the gunmen who was about to shoot. Billy squeezed the trigger and the man was knocked sideways by the impact of the bullet.

The men in the trucks noticed the shot from the Jeep. It suddenly wasn't fun anymore now that someone was shooting at them. The drivers tried to move the trucks, but they were bogged down in the sand. Trying to move them rocked them so much that the men in them could no longer shoot straight.

Ted and Jonas did not have that problem. They were focused complete on the Elders now trying to reach the wormhole. Ari-Ana's diaphanous white gown made an especially attractive target. Jonas aimed straight for her and squeezed off a shot.

Ari-Ana screamed at the pain and fell to the sand. Enela turned back for her as other shots from Ted and Jonas whizzed by her. Jonas had been watching and knew that Enela would have to stop to retrieve the one in the white gown. Of course he didn't realize that Enela had been the visitor to his house. After all, these 'jigapoos' all looked alike to him. He waited until Enela did stop then carefully aimed right at her.

The shot that came wasn't from Jonas. It came from Billy and it hit Jonas in the side of the head, splattering blood all over Ted. At that point, Ted didn't think this was much fun either. He bailed out of the car and took cover between it and the butte.

There were still a few shots from the trucks. Some of the Elders were hit. Alina was killed. One of the others picked up her body and dragged it through the wormhole. Enela and Ari-Ula were the last to reach the wormhole. They helped the others as best they could. They each took one last look around to be sure everyone had made it. Then they stepped together through the wormhole. It took another full minute for the wormhole to close.

When all of the Elders had entered the wormhole the shooting stopped. There were no more targets. From the perspective of the men in the trucks, it was not clear just what had happened to the Elders. They had simply disappeared into thin air. They continued to stare at the spot where the wormhole had been, but was not visible to anyone left on the desert floor.

Billy took advantage of the pause. He very much wanted to get his hands on those men, but he had a problem, or rather two problems. His jeep was lying on its side in the sand and he still had Agent Harris to deal with.

Billy looked at Agent Harris who was brushing the sand off his clothes. "You okay?" he asked.

"Yeah, I guess so," was the cautious response. "It's not every day that I get a roller-coaster ride in an open jeep and then get thrown out of it when it turns over."

"I want to get over there before they realize the show is over and bug out ," Billy said. He opened the toolbox in the back of the jeep and pulled out two ropes, each with a large hook attached to one end. With a practiced ease Billy fastened the hooks to the upper side of the jeep and threw one of the ropes to Agent Harris.

"Let's get this thing back on its feet," Billy said. "It usually just takes one good pull."

"I take it you've done this before?" Harris grunted as he and Billy righted the Jeep.

"A few times," Billy replied as he stowed the ropes back in the toolbox. "That's why I like this little baby."

Just as Billy and Harris had climbed back into the Jeep and started out toward the butte there was a violent and noisy explosion in the cave. The entire top of the butte was raised a few feet and then came crashing down spewing rocks and dust in its wake. Several tons of loose rock and debris came cascading down upon the trucks parked beneath the butte.

A few of the men standing in the back of the trucks had been blown clear by the force of the blast. Those inside the trucks were not so lucky. They were completely buried; the trucks crushed by the weight of the rocks.

Billy raced over to the scene, Agent Harris hanging on for dear life. But by the time they arrived it was all over. One of the men had survived with only minor injuries. Two others had severe abrasions and broken bones. One had apparent internal injuries. Gauss was dead of a gunshot wound. All of the others had died as a result of injuries suffered in the blast.

Billy called the county sheriff and asked for medical assistance. Then he did the best he could with supplies from his Jeep. Gray Wolf arrived to help with the injured. But Red Hawk had another, more urgent mission. She had not had any contact with Taka since she saw him dropping out of the sky. She knew approximately where he had landed and hurried to the spot at the northern end of the butte. There was not much damage from the blast there, so she held out hope that she could find him alive.

At first Red Hawk just looked with her eyes. She was too worried to concentrate easily. When that did not serve to find Taka, she sat down on a boulder and started searching with her mind. Still, there was no sign of Taka. Red Hawk felt a tear well from her eye and start to trickle down her cheek. She couldn't believe that Taka was gone. She just sat there quietly, one tear following the other.

"You'd better have a nice large rabbit for me after all of this bother!" It was Taka! The sudden arrival and the force of this thought jarred Red

Hawk back into the reality of the moment. She looked up and searched the sky for the source of the comment.

"Not up there. Down here!" The last two words said with a distinct tone of resignation.

Red Hawk looked down. There among the rocks, well wedged in was Taka. "Are you all right?" Red Hawk knew as soon as she said it that was the wrong question.

"Of course I'm not all right!" was the strident response. "That last shot clipped most of the feathers on my left wing. I had a heck of a time just landing in one piece. I was just sitting here on one of these rocks, out of sight of those men, trying to figure out how I could get airborne again when the whole mountain erupted and I fell down into this crevice."

Red Hawk knew just what to do. "I am glad your injury was not severe, Taka. It is the just token for fighting so brilliantly and bravely as my champion. We could never have won the battle without your help! I will see to it that you are properly rewarded and that your exploits will be told about the campfires of my people in the years to come."

"I still want my rabbit," Taka was appropriately mollified. "And I will need a safe place to stay until my feathers repair themselves."

"You can stay with Gray Wolf, Taka. He will see that you are properly cared for and have your fill of mice and rabbits. Come, climb on my arm and I will take you to his cabin."

Red Hawk removed her dress and wrapped it about her arm so that Taka would have a secure perch. Then the two of them made their way back

227

to Gray Wolf's cabin, avoiding the scene of carnage on the other side of the butte.

It took the sheriff and several paramedics some time to clear the scene of the battle. Billy was quite clear about having seen the whole thing. How these men had come out from the town to do a little target shooting and had selected a group of reservation children as their targets. Thanks to the timely arrival and intervention of Billy and Agent Harris, none of the children were hurt and had all fled back to their homes. No, Billy couldn't identify any of them right off hand, but he would ask around. Yes, he was sure that none of them were hurt. The explosion? Well, Billy admitted that he had been storing some old dynamite in a cave up on the other side of the butte. A stray shot must have set it off. Pity, but just retribution for such a heinous act as shooting at a bunch of kids.

When he was asked, Agent Harris had to admit that he was bouncing around so violently in the Jeep that he couldn't see much of anything. But the men were definitely shooting at a bunch of small people. Children as likely as not. Then he admitted to being face down in the sand when Billy was shooting back. He just didn't see a thing.

Billy didn't know quite whether to believe him or not, but he was thankful for the agent's support. When the sheriff and the medics had cleared out with the remnants of Gauss's hunting team, Billy was faced with the last, and greatest question.

"Still want to investigate the cave?" he asked.

Harris looked up at the butte in the fading light and took his time answering. "I don't see any cave up there. Doesn't look like there is anything left to investigate. But, if I were you, I would look for a better place to store old dynamite in the future. Might be some innocent mountain climbers will stumble on it next time …"

Billy did his best to stifle the sigh of relief that seemed to well up involuntarily. He and Agent Harris drove back to Wakulla in silence.

Epilogue

"I must report that Taka did not suffer any permanent physical injury," Red Hawk said. "Only his pride was deeply wounded. It took several rounds of encouragement and praise to build back his ego. It seems that just like males of the human species, the males of the great hawk species have very fragile egos.

"Gray Wolf managed to glue some pieces of feathers back onto the stubs left by the bullets. In a few days, and after some rather humorous attempts trying, Taka was again soaring through the sky. Of course, as his own feathers grew out, he had to return to Gray Wolf for an occasional trimming of the add-ons.

"Agent Harris was true to his word. The FBI never came back to inquire into the cave in the butte. I do not know what happened to Agent Askins. I imagine he had to answer a lot of questions. We never saw either of them again.

"Mary presented a difficult problem. When her father ran out of her room she grabbed some clothes and bailed out the window after Enela. She saw Enela driving off in her father's car and figured out what had happened. Mary hid out behind the house until her father had departed with his Lodge brothers. Then she went back in the house and tried to figure out what to do. She was still there when a deputy sheriff arrived to tell her about her father's death. The double loss of Enela and her father drove Mary into a deep depression.

Enela had told Mary about me and how I had helped her get over some of her problems. Mary soon came to me for help. It didn't take too long to get Mary straightened out. Then it was a matter of deciding what to do with her life. After some dickering we decided that I would petition the court to have Mary declared an emancipated minor. She was almost of legal age anyway, and I knew a few influential people, so that was quickly done. She had plenty of money left over from the taxi business and a fine home to live in. Everything seemed to be going just fine.

"I got busy for a while and did not talk to Mary for several months. When I went to her high school graduation I learned that she had already taken her diploma and left town. Her house was subsequently sold and I lost touch with her. I did not see Mary again for a very long time.

"The matter of Enela and Ari-Ana requires some explanation.

"When I first started working with Enela I put her into a deep trance and started delving into her race memory to see if I could find a cause for her problems adjusting to Elder life. At first I found the same conditions that I had found with all of the other Elders. With them the race memory seemed to end at the point at which they arrived on our planet. Enela, on the other hand, had memories that went back beyond her ancestors' arrival on earth. She could actually remember life as it had been on her home world.

"This was astounding and I reported all of my findings to Ari-Ana as I had been asked to do. Enela was always in a trance while I was working with her and I carefully ensured that she did not remember the outcome of any of our sessions. I assumed that she could recall her own race memories should she have the need to do so, but I didn't want to burden her unnecessarily with what I had learned.

"What I did learn caused Ari-Ana to have serious doubts about the plan to return to the Elders' home world. For whatever reason, she chose not to tell the other councilors exactly what I had discovered, but encouraged them to reconsider their plan. Without the details, the other councilors refused to listen to Ari-Ana and proceeded with the plan to use the wormhole.

"Whether things would have been different if Enela and Mary had never met, or if her father had not been such a bigot, I can not say. What I can say is that all of the original Elders left our time without any plan or known ability ever to return."

== 30 ==

Also by Robyn Kelly:

The Elder Chronicles: The Lost World
The Elder Chronicles: Birth of a Savior
The Elder Chronicles: Elder Child
The Elder Chronicles: The Legend of Red Hawk

Watch for volume six
The Elder Chronicles: A New Breed
Coming Soon!